"How far along are you?" Ethan asked, his tone deceptively mild.

"Ten weeks." Sloane watched him closely while he flashed through the math, waiting to see anger light his eyes, denial tighten his jaw. She didn't see either of those emotions, though. Instead, there was something else, something she had no idea how to read.

He set his shoulders. "Is it mine?"

She nodded, suddenly unable to find words. Hormones, she thought as tears sprang to her eyes. Stupid pregnancy hormones.

Wonderful, Ethan thought. That made two women he'd driven to tears that week.

He hadn't expected this. Not once, in all the times that he'd thought of Sloane, had he imagined that their one night together had led to a baby. A baby that was half Hartwell genes.

Half a potential for such a disaster that his breath came short.

Dear Reader,

Over the years, I've worked as a librarian, a lawyer, a ski-school receptionist, a database-maintenance engineer, a summer-camp drama specialist and many other things. My favorite job though (aside from writing full time!) was working as a salesclerk in a bookstore.

Working every day, surrounded by some of my favorite books, I realized that I wanted to write a Harlequin romance novel. I read every one that I could get my hands on, month after month after month. I wrote one, only to realize that it wasn't good enough to submit. I wrote another, and I was pleased to find that it was better, but still not ready for prime time. I wrote a third, sent it in and was crestfallen when it was rejected.

Along the way, I attended more school and I took on other careers. I published twelve other novels. But I always longed to achieve that initial dream, to return to my Harlequin writing roots.

And now, many years after I first tried my hand at literary matchmaking, I can finally share this novel with you. Ethan and Sloane's story was a long time coming, and I hope that you'll find it was worth the wait!

I love to hear from my readers—please stop by and visit me at www.mindyklasky.com.

All best wishes,

Mindy

THE MOGUL'S MAYBE MARRIAGE

MINDY KLASKY

Harlequin®

SPECIAL EDITION

Recycling programs
for this product may
not exist in your area.

ISBN-13: 978-0-373-65617-2

THE MOGUL'S MAYBE MARRIAGE

MINDY KLASKY

learned to read when her parents shoved a book in her hands and told her that she could travel anywhere in the world through stories. She never forgot that advice. These days, Mindy works and plays in a suburb of Washington, D.C., where she lives with her family. In her spare time, Mindy knits, cooks and tries to tame the endless to-be-read shelf in her home library. You can visit Mindy at her website, www.mindyklasky.com.

To my fellow Arent Fox summer associates—
who laughed with me as Sloane was born

Chapter One

Ethan Hartwell was not accustomed to waiting.

He glanced over in annoyance, not bothering to hide the action from the sour-faced assistant who guarded the inner office. His BlackBerry buzzed and he accepted another appointment for that afternoon. He forwarded a scheduling notice about his Seattle trip the following week.

Hartwell Genetics couldn't afford to get left behind, not with domestic and international demand exploding for the company's gene-based medicines.

If he was going to be kept waiting like a recalcitrant schoolboy outside the principal's office, then he might as well get his homework done.

Another buzz. More email. Ethan cleared his throat to get the attention of the gray-haired Gorgon. "I'm going back to my office," he said.

Before he could carry through on the threat, the door

guard raised a talon to her ear. She nodded at whatever secret message she received, then leveled cold eyes toward Ethan before intoning, "You may go in now."

Games. If he'd announced his decision to leave fifteen minutes earlier, then he would have been granted admittance that much sooner. He shoved his BlackBerry onto his hip and twitched the legs of his trousers into perfect place. For full effect, he shot the cuffs of his shirt, making sure that his wristwatch glinted in the overhead lights. He told himself that his deep breath was to complete the image, to cement the vision of Ethan Hartwell, M.D., MBA, third-generation president of Hartwell Genetics and the most eligible bachelor of Washington, D.C., for three years running.

In reality, he merely needed a moment to clear his head before he entered the inner sanctum.

The handle turned smoothly under his lean fingers, and the door glided open in silence. Ethan's black wingtips left deep impressions in the cream carpet as he crossed the room. He ignored the framed pictures on the wall, photographs taken with the President, with political and business leaders from throughout the civilized world. The United States Capitol was centered in the picture window behind the massive mahogany desk, as perfect as a movie backdrop. With the force of long habit, Ethan crossed behind that desk, approaching the imposing throne that housed the office's lone occupant.

He bent at the waist and settled a faint kiss on a cheek that smelled of baby powder and lilacs. "Good morning, Grandmother," Ethan said.

Margaret Hartwell's eyes gleamed like agate chips as she waved him to one of her uncomfortable Louis XIV chairs. "Will you join me for a cup of tea?"

Ethan swallowed a sigh. It was faster to accept his

grandmother's hospitality than to argue with her. He poured with the ease of familiarity, placing a gleaming strainer across her china cup, dropping in two cubes of sugar, adding a generous dollop of milk. He took his own black, strong and bitter. Determined to conclude their conversation and get back to work, he said, "Grandmother—"

"I finished reading the newspaper this morning, before I came into the office," she interrupted.

He, too, had skimmed the *Wall Street Journal* and the *Financial Times* while his chauffeured car had been stuck in morning traffic. "The new treatment is performing well," he said. "We should move on to stage-two trials next month."

As if he needed to tell his grandmother about pharmaceutical development. As Hartwell Genetics's former president and current chairman of the board, Margaret Hartwell chased down medical news like a ravenous greyhound. Maybe that was why she had the capacity to annoy him so much—they were too much alike: driven, determined and downright dogged about pursuing every last business lead.

"I'm not speaking about stage-two trials," she said acerbically. "I was referring to the gossip page."

Ethan raised one eyebrow. He and his grandmother might be united on the business front, but they were miles apart where his personal life was concerned. "Grandmother, we've had this discussion before. You know that I can't control what the papers print."

She settled her teacup in her saucer with a firm clink. "You *can* control the fodder you give those imbeciles. I've told you until I'm blue in the face—your actions have a direct effect on this company."

He shoved his teacup away. "I hardly think that my

drinking champagne on a hotel rooftop is going to influence our second quarter earnings."

"She's a *showgirl*, Ethan."

He laughed and rose to his feet. "There haven't been showgirls since you were a debutante, Grandmother. Natasha is an *actress*. And don't worry. She flew back to California this morning."

"You will *not* walk out of my office while I am talking to you!"

He shouldn't have been surprised by the iron in his grandmother's voice. He knew that he brought out the worst in her, and vice versa, for that matter. All of a sudden, he was an abandoned little boy again, being chastised by the only relative who had stuck around to raise him. He was the sixteen-year-old who had been expelled from Washington's finest private school—again—for playing tricks with the headmaster's public address system. He was the twenty-year-old who had been thrown off the college tennis team for sneaking his girlfriend into the tournament locker room. He was the twenty-seven-year-old who had celebrated receiving his medical degree and his business degree on the same day, only to crash his Porsche into the Tidal Basin.

He was the thirty-three-year-old corporate executive, standing before his chairman of the board.

"Ethan, enough is enough. Your parties and your women are bringing down this company. They're distracting you. And they're not even making you happy." His grandmother gave him the flinty stare that had sealed a thousand legendary business deals. "Ethan, I want you married by no later than my birthday."

He laughed.

"This isn't a joke." She leaned forward across her desk. All of a sudden, Ethan became aware of the deep lines beside her mouth, the bags beneath her eyes. Her fingers were knotted as she laid them flat against her gold-scrolled leather blotter. Did they tremble because she was angry with him? Or was something more going on? He barely resisted the urge to reach across her desk, to fold his fingers around the pulse point in her wrist, to measure her heart rate. Was she keeping track of her medication? Was she managing the high blood pressure?

"Grandmother," he said, purposely striving for a soothing tone. "I'm a grown man. I'll decide when it's time to marry."

"I wish I believed that." Her voice quaked, spiking his own blood with a touch of true concern. "I've tried to be patient, Ethan, but I'm terrified that I'll die without knowing our family will continue." She raised one trembling hand to silence his automatic protest. "I know that you're afraid. But we can *test* now. We can be absolutely certain that any child you father is spared the genetic mutation."

He had never seen his grandmother cry before. Not when two grandchildren had died—Ethan's siblings. Not when Ethan's mourning parents had incinerated their marriage. Not when Grandmother had been left with the responsibility of managing the company that the family had originally founded to research an end to their long-kept medical secret. Not when she had buried her beloved husband of fifty-one years.

But she was crying now.

"You have a responsibility, Ethan. To the Hartwell family and to this company. To yourself. It's time for you to settle down." She must have read the automatic rebellion in his expression. She sat up straighter, staring at him with the hazel eyes that were the more benign manifestation of his Hartwell heritage. "And if you're not willing to do that, then I'll have no choice but to step down from the board and transfer my shares in Hartwell Genetics."

Her shares. Enough stock to influence every major corporate decision. If someone else owned Grand-mother's interest, Ethan would be forced to fight, to keep the secret of his own genetic heritage. He'd be bound to waste countless hours cajoling along new business colleagues, educating them about the corporation's diverse pharmaceutical initiatives, all the while keeping secret its one dear mission. Ethan could kiss every one of his short-term goals goodbye while he adjusted to the change. And under a new regime, his long-term plans might never coalesce.

"You don't mean that," he said.

"I do. I need to know that I've built *something* that will last, Ethan, something that will outlive me." He heard every one of her seventy-nine years in her voice. "Ethan, I need to know that you can step up to your obligations. That you will guide Hartwell Genetics through its next fifty years. If you can't prove that to me—if you're not married by January fifth—then I'm celebrating eight decades by transferring my entire estate to the American Foundation for the Advancement of the Arts."

AFAA. His grandmother's longtime pet charity.

This was even worse than he'd thought a moment ago. AFAA had no interest in medicine. They would view a massive infusion of corporate stock as a conservative investment. They would do their best to challenge every decision Ethan made to expand the corporate mission, to bring Hartwell Genetics into new markets. They'd argue for safety and security and preservation of their newfound wealth, at all costs.

Ethan sighed. He'd escorted Grandmother to the foundation's annual charity auction only a couple of months before, at the luxurious Eastern Hotel, the one with the bar that overlooked the Washington Monument.

He swallowed hard, his mouth suddenly dry. He'd bought a drink for the auction coordinator that night. A drink, and then a hastily arranged suite on the penthouse level of the hotel.

Sloane. Sloane Davenport.

He could still see Sloane's delicate, self-conscious smile as she admitted that she'd never done anything like that before, never gone off with a man she'd just met. He had silenced her confession with a kiss, not willing to admit to himself just how much her innocence attracted him, how much her shyness drew him in.

Since the auction, he'd picked up the phone to call her half a dozen times, but he'd never followed through. He hadn't wanted to hear regret when he identified himself. Hadn't wanted to think about the conversation they'd shared in the dark, the talk that had gone on, sleepy and comfortable, long after their bodies were sated. Hadn't wanted to remember waking up alone, with just a memory of her honeysuckle scent on the pillow.

He cleared his throat and shifted his weight, ordering his body to relax, to forget the only night that stood out from the past year's slideshow of one-night stands. "AFAA," he finally forced himself to say.

His grandmother's eyes glittered as she tapped a thick manila folder on her desk. "I have the papers here, Ethan. Zach drew them up."

Zach Crosby. Ethan's best friend. His grandmother's personal attorney.

Ethan turned on his heel and left, ignoring his grandmother's sharp remonstration, ignoring her secretary's petulant frown, ignoring the buzz of his BlackBerry.

Seven months to find a bride. And he had absolutely no doubt that his grandmother would follow through on her threat if he failed. He was certain of that. She loved him, and she would do whatever she thought best to save him. Even if he didn't want to be saved.

Sloane Davenport gasped as her computer screen flickered, giving one heart-stopping moment of blue-screen warning before it died. Damn! That was the third time today. And she had no way of knowing if her email had been sent before the stupid machine crashed. No way of knowing if her résumé was heading out toward a prospective new employer. No way of knowing if she might finally be making her way out of the mess that enveloped her.

She stood slowly, bracing her palms against the kitchen table before she folded her fingers into fists and rubbed the small of her back. The dull, throbbing pain had returned. She grimaced and picked up a saltine from her chipped plate. Nausea swirled through her belly, but she forced herself to chew slowly, to swallow an entire glass of water when she was done.

Two and a half months. She should be past the morning sickness any day now. That's what the book said, the dog-eared volume that she kept on her coffee table like a family Bible.

She shrugged and reached for the stack of papers beside her computer. Bills. Fortunately, she kept her checkbook on paper. No chance for her ancient computer to ruin *them*.

Not that the curling slips of paper offered any great comfort. At least she'd managed to send her rent check on time. She glanced at the air conditioner that chugged along in the kitchen window of her tiny basement apartment. Her landlord covered utilities. No need to worry about electricity or water.

Student loans, though, were another matter. She'd sent off a tiny payment, along with a note explaining that she'd send more, as soon as she was able.

Like *that* was going to happen anytime soon. Expenses related to the baby had barely begun, and Sloane was already overwhelmed. Soon, she was going to have to buy some new clothes. She wasn't showing yet, but it was only a matter of weeks. Her jeans were already snug in the waistband, and she'd left the button unfastened as she worked at her kitchen table.

She'd have to get some decent groceries, too, as soon as she could keep down more than crackers and ramen noodles. For now, she had to hope that her expensive prenatal vitamins were doing their job. She glared at the white bottle on the counter.

And she'd have to scrape together money for a doctor.

She'd fit in her first prenatal visit just before her insurance ran out. Two months had gone by, though, two visits that she owed herself, owed her baby. She tried to believe that she could wait until she had a new job, until she was insured, but as every day passed without her landing a new position, she became more and more afraid.

She rubbed her fingers across the thin fabric of her T-shirt, letting them curl over the tiny life that lurked inside. Would she have handled things differently with AFAA, if she'd known that she was pregnant?

Her cheeks flushed as she remembered taking the subway home from the Eastern that morning after the auction. She had tottered down the steps to her apartment, her feet pinched in unaccustomed high heels.

Despite her exhaustion, despite the awkwardness of slipping out of the hotel suite unseen and unheard, despite the heart-catching memories from the night before that kept drowning her, she'd caught herself with a goofy smile on her face. She had sung out loud in the shower as she got ready for work. Silly songs. Love songs.

Oh, she knew that Ethan Hartwell didn't love her. He *couldn't* love her. He was famous and rich and the toast of the gossiping town.

But there had been *something* in his eyes when he'd come to stand beside her at the bar, where she'd granted herself a well-deserved break after managing the most successful fundraising auction in AFAA history. There'd been something in the set of his jaw as he gestured for the bartender to make her another vodka gimlet. Something in the curve of his lips as they bantered, as she flirted.

As *she* flirted…

Sloane sighed, remembering how easily the words had come to her, as if she were blessed by some daring goddess of romance. For once in her life, it had been simple to talk to a man, to tease him, to taunt. A little amazed, she'd watched Ethan lean close to her. She'd lowered her voice, bit her lip, dipped her head. When he'd settled a finger on her chin, raising her face to his, she'd felt the promise radiating from his hand. She'd registered the heat that had cascaded over her body in a sudden, astonishing wave.

She'd tasted whiskey on his lips, smoky liquor that swirled through the clean citrus tang of her own drink. Without conscious thought, she'd drunk in more of the flavor of his cocktail, of him. The touch of his tongue on hers had sent an electric tingle down her spine, and she'd shuddered, grateful for his firm hand on the small of her back, steadying her, drawing her closer.

One hour, another drink and much banter later, he'd turned away to the bartender, said something that she couldn't quite catch. She'd seen the flash of a silver credit card pass between the men, and minutes later, the exchange of a plastic room key.

Another kiss had sealed his invitation, that one rocketing across the tender velvet of her mouth, curling through her belly, trembling into the vulnerable flesh behind her knees. She'd found some witty words to reply, and then she was grateful for the fiery hand that he cupped against her nape, for the scorching iron of his body next to hers as he led the way across the bar, to the elevator, to the penthouse suite that he had so effortlessly secured.

His ease had given her the confidence to do all the things she wanted to do. She didn't need to wonder if she should say *this,* if she should do *that.* Instead, she'd trusted herself. She'd trusted him. For one perfect night, she was more comfortable than she'd ever been with a man. It was more than just the sex, more than the amazing things he made her body feel. They had actually *talked,* hour after hour, lying next to each other in the dark, sharing stories of their very different pasts. Everything just felt…right.

In the morning, though, she'd snuck out before he was awake. That's what women did—at least according to movies, according to the newspapers, to the tabloids that feasted on men like Bachelor of the Year Ethan Hartwell. She'd snuck out, gone home to shower, made it in to the office no more than thirty minutes late.

Thirty minutes that her boss had spent waiting for

her. Thirty minutes that he'd spent building a furious argument.

Didn't Sloane know that AFAA had an image to uphold? AFAA project coordinators could not fraternize with prominent playboy bachelors in public bars where donors—discerning donors, *conservative* donors—could see them. AFAA project coordinators certainly could not slink off with their conquests, leaving nothing to the imagination about their destination. AFAA project coordinators could never threaten the long-term success of an organization as traditional and staid and sedate as the foundation—not when offended donors threatened to rescind their pledged funds because of the immoral behavior of AFAA staff.

AFAA project coordinators could be replaced without a second's hesitation.

Even now, weeks later, Sloane grimaced at the memory.

Before she could collect her notes and head to the library with its working computer terminal, her doorbell rang, making her jump in surprise. She never had visitors. When she looked through the peephole, she nearly sank to the floor in disbelief.

Ethan Hartwell. As if she had summoned him with her recollection of that one night.

That was absurd, though. She'd thought about that night almost nonstop since March. Mere *thought* had never brought Ethan to her door before.

Heart pounding, she ran her fingers through her hair. Thank goodness she'd taken a shower that morning, brushed her teeth, even remembered to floss. She glanced down at her trim navy T-shirt, took a second to fiddle with the button on her jeans, sucking in her breath to camouflage her incipient baby bump. He couldn't tell, could he? Not yet. No one could, she reasoned with herself.

The doorbell rang again, long and insistent. She set her jaw against the demand. What did Ethan Hartwell want with her? Why had he come now? She thought about not answering, about letting him go away. He could phone her, if he really needed her. Her number was listed.

But then, she remembered his hazel eyes, the ones that had first snagged her attention at the Eastern. She remembered his rich voice, reverberating to the marrow of her bones. She remembered his broad palms, curving around her hips, pulling her closer....

She threw open the double locks, just as he was raising his fist to knock.

"Ethan," she said, proud that her voice was steady, bright, with just the perfect brush of surprise.

"Sloane." He lowered his hand to his side. His eyes flared as he took in her face, as if he were confirming a memory. He licked his lips, and then he produced the same devastating smile that had completely sunk her back at the hotel. "May I come in?"

Silently, she stepped to the side. She caught his scent as he strode past her, something like pine needles under moonlight, something utterly, completely male. She waited for a familiar twist of nausea to leap up at the aroma, but she was pleasantly surprised to find that her belly remained calm.

Not that her body didn't react to him. Her lips tingled as she sucked in a steadying breath. Her heart raced enough that she half expected him to turn around, to glare at her chest, disturbed by the noise. The thought of his eyes on her chest only stirred her more. She bit her lip as her nipples tightened into pearls, and she crossed her arms over the navy jersey of her shirt.

Faking a tiny cough, she asked, "Can I get you something to drink?" She couldn't make him coffee. She didn't trust her rebellious stomach around the smell as it brewed. "Some tea?" she asked.

He shook his head. "No," he said. "I'm fine." He strode to her couch as if he owned the place.

She'd lived in the apartment for nearly three years. In all that time, she'd never realized how small the space really was, how little air there was in the room. She watched his gaze dart toward the diminutive kitchen, to the tiny table with its mismatched pair of chairs, to the narrow counter. He glanced toward her bedroom, and she had a sudden vision of him literally sweeping her off her feet, carrying her through the doorway, easing her onto the double bed's crumpled sheets.

She flexed her fingers and reminded herself to breathe. Gesturing at the living room, she said, "Not quite the Eastern, is it?"

He ignored her question. "You left the foundation."

She bridled at his tone. "I didn't think I needed your permission to change jobs."

He ignored her sarcasm. "I tried to reach you there, yesterday morning. All they'd say was that you left a couple of months ago. I guess the auction was your last fling?"

She flushed. He had no way of knowing that the night they'd spent together was special to her. Precious, in a way that words could never make him understand. Her vulnerability rasped an undertone of challenge across her voice. "Why do you care? Why were you calling me, anyway?"

In the dim light, his hazel eyes looked black. "Your

name came up in conversation. I wondered how you were doing."

"My name came up," she said, fighting a tangle of disbelief and excitement. "After two and half months? Just like that?" She hated the fact that her voice shook on the last word.

He closed the distance between them, settling a hand on her arm. She knew that she should pull away, keep a safe distance. But she didn't entirely trust her suddenly trembling legs.

"Let's try this again," he said. "Sit down." He must have heard the note of command beneath his words, because he inclined his head and gestured toward the sofa as if it were something elegant, something worthy of royalty. "Please."

She took a seat, pretending that the action was her own idea, even as she was grateful for the support against her back. She longed to cradle one of the throw pillows in her lap, to hide behind the cushion. Instead, she folded her hands across her belly, trying to summon a calm that she could not feel past her pounding heart. As he sat beside her, she tried to think of something to say, anything, some everyday conversational gambit that would pass for normal between two consenting adults.

He spoke before she did, though, his tone deceptively mild. "How far along are you?"

She clutched at her T-shirt. "How did you know?"

"The vitamins." He nodded toward her kitchen counter, toward the white plastic bottle that announced its contents in bright orange letters. "The book." She blushed as his gaze fell on the coffee table. He insisted, "How many weeks?"

"Ten." She watched him closely while he flashed through the math, waiting to see anger light his eyes, denial tighten his jaw. She didn't see either of those emotions, though. Instead, there was something else, something she had no idea how to read.

He set his shoulders. "Is it mine?"

She nodded, suddenly unable to find words. Hormones, she thought as tears sprang to her eyes. Stupid pregnancy hormones.

Wonderful, Ethan thought. That made two women he'd driven to tears that week.

He hadn't expected this. Not once, in all the times that he'd thought of Sloane, had he imagined that their one night together had led to a baby. A baby that was half Hartwell genes. Half a potential for such a disaster that his breath came short.

They'd used protection, of course. He wasn't an idiot. But he *was* a doctor, and he knew the statistics. Condoms failed, three percent of the time. Three percent, and after a lifetime of luck, of practice, of protection, he'd just lost the lottery.

He had come to Sloane that morning with mixed emotions, determined to maintain his independence, even as he gave lip service to his grandmother's edict. He had thought that he and Sloane could get to know each other better. After all, in the past year, she'd been the only woman he'd thought about once he'd left her bed. The only woman he'd ever wanted to confide something in, confide *everything* in. Which, of course, had made him vow never to contact her again.

Except now he needed a woman. He needed a *wife.* And Sloane had been the first person to cross his mind when Grandmother issued her ultimatum.

He had fooled himself, thinking that everything would be simple. They could go out on a few proper dates. Stay out of bed, difficult as that might prove to be. Even as Ethan had built his plan, he'd been wryly amused by the thought that Sloane worked at AFAA. If, after a month or two of testing the waters, he found that he and Sloane truly *were* compatible, then she would be the perfect ironic tool to rein in his grandmother's plan. He would put a ring on Sloane's finger, and AFAA would lose the potential for a controlling interest in Hartwell Genetics.

Except the stakes had just been raised. Astronomically. And Sloane didn't have the least idea what was going on. She had no concept of what heartbreak her future might bear. Ethan set his jaw. There were tests, as his grandmother had reminded him. Tests that could be run as soon as Sloane reached her fourteenth week.

He'd let the silence stretch out too long between them. He had to know. "You're alone here?"

Again, she nodded. He tried to identify the emotions that swirled into his relief at that saving grace: pleasure, coupled with a surprisingly fierce possessiveness. She was alone. *Unattached,* he knew they both meant.

"Good," he growled.

The single word sparked a fire beneath Sloane's heart. Sure, she'd dreamed about sharing her news with him. She'd written silly scenes inside her head, of Ethan finding her a few years from now, after she had built a career, had proved to herself and the rest of the world that she was strong and independent. She had let herself fill in the impossible details— she would be playing in the park with their baby, their happy and carefree and perfect child, when Ethan just happened to walk by, taking a stroll on a brilliant spring morning.

But in her heart of hearts, she had known that could never happen. Ethan would never be there for her, would never share this baby with her. They'd only spent one night together, and they'd taken every precaution to make sure that she would never end up in this precise condition.

Besides, she'd done her research after the night they'd spent together, following up on all the gossip that she had vaguely recalled when she saw him at the Eastern bar. She had forced herself to read the articles about his playboy lifestyle, the stream of women in his life, the flirtations that splashed across the society page.

Sloane's daydreams had to be impossible. Right?

"Sloane," he said, breaking into her swirling thoughts. "I should have been in touch before. I know this sounds sudden, but I've been thinking about you since that night. A lot. When I woke and you had left, I figured that I would accept what you obviously wanted."

He reached out and settled his broad hand across her belly. The tips of his fingers ignited tiny fires beneath her shirt, and she caught her breath in pleasure and surprise. He flexed his wrist, using the motion to glide near, to close the distance between them. "But everything is different now."

His mouth on hers was unexpected. She felt the power within him, a coil of energy. Her body reacted before her mind could parcel out a well-reasoned response. She leaned toward him, drawn to his touch like a starving woman to a feast. His tongue traced the line between her lips, and she yielded without any conscious decision. Her fingers fluttered from the shelter of her lap, tangled in his hair, pulled him closer to her.

The motion of her hands seemed to free his own; his fingers were suddenly hot as they slipped beneath her T-shirt, searing as they danced across her still-flat belly. He cupped one sensitive breast with his hand, rasping the lace of her bra against her flesh. Her body had never been so responsive, and she gasped in surprise. She folded her fingers over his. "Just a moment."

Ethan dropped his head to her shoulder, cradling his cheek against the pulse that pounded by her ear.

This was madness. He'd come here, planning on being the perfect gentleman. He'd intended to wind back the clock, to give them both time to get to know each other, space to explore their true potential together. He'd meant to build on the amazing foundation they'd established back at the Eastern, that endless night of talking and loving and talking some more.

He couldn't help himself, though. Even knowing that she was carrying his baby. *Especially* knowing that.

He tensed his arms and pushed himself away just enough that he could look into her eyes, into a blue so deep that he felt like he was drowning. He spoke before he even knew that he was going to say the words. "Sloane. Marry me."

"What?" Sloane couldn't believe that she had heard him right. He reached out to trace a finger along her lips, but she turned her head aside. How could he have read her daydreams? How could he have known the secret stories that she told herself, just as she was drifting off to sleep?

"Marry me," he said again, as if those two words made all the sense in the world.

He couldn't mean it.

Sure, she'd imagined him proposing, once he found out the truth about their single night together. She'd pictured red roses and dry champagne, a sparkling diamond ring fresh out of some teenager's fantasy.

But in her dreams, they had known each other for longer before he proposed. They had indulged in a thousand conversations, countless discoveries of every last thing they had in common. They had filled days —and nights—with laughter, with secrets. They had built a flawless base for their future. He had left behind his reputation for womanizing, finally content to stay with one true...love?

That was all a wonderful dream. But dreams never did come true. Certainly not *her* dreams, not the dreams of a foster kid who'd spent a lifetime being shifted from unloving home to unloving home. Her old defensiveness kicked in just in time to save her, to remind her that she had to protect herself and her baby, that no one else would ever do that as well as she could. She tugged her shirt back into place, willing her flesh to stop tingling. Roughening her voice, she demanded, "Are you insane?"

His eyes flashed as he drew himself to his feet, and she tried to read the expression on his face. Guilt. Or embarrassment. "I'm trying to do the right thing," he said, his voice strained.

She wanted to believe him. She wanted to think that this could really be happening to her. But seriously. Ethan Hartwell? Hartwell Genetics billionaire? Bachelor of the Year?

Her silence seemed to feed something within him, something angry and hard. His jaw tightened. He reached into his back pocket and pulled out a sleek wallet. Two fingers scissored out a business card, a perfect white rectangle. He crossed to her kitchen table, and she tried to read what he was thinking from the tense lines of his back.

His eyes were hooded when he turned around to face her. "Think about it, Sloane. I want to do what's right. A paternity test, and then a proper wedding. You won't get a better offer." He didn't wait for her to reply. Instead, he let himself out the door, closing it with a crisp finality.

He truly *must* be nuts. One minute, he was the astonishing, charming man she'd met at the Eastern, the man who had convinced her to spend the night with him, all because of his easy smile, because of the instant kinship that had sparked between them.

The next minute, though, he was a cold professional. A doctor and a businessman, driving a hard corporate bargain. Demanding a paternity test! He didn't believe her. He thought that someone else could be the father, that she made a habit of picking up random men in hotel bars.

She'd show him. She'd take that business card and tear it into a hundred pieces. She'd flush it down the toilet. She'd grind it up in the garbage disposal. She stormed into the tiny kitchen.

Her tirade was cut short, though, drowned by the sight that met her astonished eyes.

Ethan's business card was centered on her dead laptop. Beneath it were five crisp hundred-dollar bills.

Five hundred dollars. More money than she'd seen since AFAA had kicked her out the door. Money that Ethan had no obligation to leave. Money that he could have made conditional, could have held out to demand her submission.

In one heartbeat, Sloane's anger turned to shame. Really, what reason did Ethan *have* to believe her, about paternity or anything else?

Sure, they'd shared the most intimate night two people could share. She was carrying a baby as proof. But had she found the courage to contact him in the intervening ten weeks? Had she summoned the internal strength to reach out to her baby's father, to tell him the truth? What if Ethan hadn't come to her that morning? How much longer would he have gone on, not knowing? Weeks? Months? Years?

All things considered, Ethan had actually reacted quite well.

What had he just said? He wanted to do what was *right*. Even after she had shut him out. Even after she had kept him from learning the truth. His first instinct had been to take care of her. To take care of their baby. He'd acted nothing like the playboy she'd read about, nothing like the man-about-town who was splashed across the gossip sheets.

Tenderness blossomed inside Sloane's chest, unfolding like a snow-white rosebud. There *was* something between them, some emotion stronger than all the half-truths, deeper than all the avoidance and uncertainty.

The corners of her lips turned up as she heard his earnest tone. *Marry me.*

Could he really mean it? Did she dare say yes?

She didn't have any model in her past for *marriage*. She hadn't grown up with a happy mother and father, with the sort of easy family life that she dreamed about after watching movies, after reading books. She couldn't imagine what it would be like to trust someone enough to want to spend the rest of her life with him.

To love someone that much.

Oh, it was far too soon to say that she loved Ethan. She knew that. But she could say that she was powerfully drawn to him. That he made her feel safe. Protected. And, more than that, he made her feel desirable. Desired. He made her feel more alive than she ever had before.

Biting her lip, Sloane picked up the five crisp bills and folded them lengthwise, creasing them between her thumb and index finger. The sleek business card continued to glint its challenge from the table's surface.

Did she have the courage to make the phone call? Did she have the strength to reach out to Ethan, to tell him what she was thinking? After a lifetime of tamping down any strong emotion, of shutting down her feelings to protect herself, could she possibly take the next step?

Chapter Two

He'd made a complete mess of that.

From the instant that Ethan settled into the back of his chauffeured Town Car, he knew that he'd made a horrible mistake.

But something about Sloane made him lose his famous business composure, softened his infinitely sharp entrepreneurial edge. *"Marry me."* Where the hell had that come from? The words had been out of his mouth before he could think how abrupt they would sound to Sloane. He'd been filled with the thought of Sloane carrying his child. He'd been captivated by the notion that all of this was *meant* to be—the one incredible night they'd spent together, the pregnancy that had resulted. His grandmother's ultimatum.

Fresh from his grandmother's office the day before, Ethan had phoned AFAA, only to find that Sloane had left the organization. His next call had been to his pri-

vate investigator. In less than twenty-four hours, Ethan
knew that Sloane had been fired. At least he had her
home address. And a credit report that told him she was
in dire need of assistance. Only one piece of data had
been missing—the pregnancy…

Ethan's plan had made so much sense. Tweak his
grandmother and her ridiculous notions of marital pro-
priety, at the same time that he figured out if there really *was* something there with Sloane.

But all those calculations had flown out the window
when he'd actually seen Sloane standing in the doorway. When he'd looked into those ocean eyes, acknowl-
edged the flash of surprise as she greeted him. The hint
of uncertainty. The sudden flicker of arousal that beck-
oned to his own scarcely banked flames. He'd watched
the blush paint her cheeks when he stepped inside the
apartment, when she crossed her arms over her chest,
trying to hide her body's blatant response to him.

And that was before he'd realized that she was pregnant.

Marry me. He'd said it, just like that. Out of the blue,
without any prelude, any explanation whatsoever. He
hadn't even taken the time to tell her that she wasn't just
one of his flings, that she was *different*. He hadn't told
her that they had connected on some level that he'd always thought was imaginary. Their midnight conversation had been the sort of thing that women read about in
their pink-and-lace books, watched in their silly damp-
handkerchief movies. It couldn't be real.

But it was.

Even now, he could remember every word they'd
shared. He'd told her about Hartwell Genetics, about
how he wanted the company to continue growing, to
change the world. How he longed to help millions with

the cures his empire was developing. How he loved the challenge, the struggle, the fierce competition in the often-ruthless business world.

And she'd told him her own dreams. What did she call it? The Hope Project, the website she wanted to build. Art therapy. Foster kids. He'd been truly touched by her unwavering determination, by her certainty that she could make a difference.

He couldn't go back now and reduce all that to nothing. He couldn't admit that his grandmother had ordered him to take a wife. And he definitely couldn't tell her the real reason for his demand, for the so-called paternity test. He'd never told anyone about the family curse, about the brother and sister who had each died before their third birthday.

No. He'd proposed, and then he'd left his ugly cash lying on the table. As if he could buy her. As if he could make Sloane do whatever he wanted her to do.

He swore, wondering how a man who was a proven genius in the business world could make such a spectacular mess out of his personal life. There had to be a way to make Sloane understand. A way to take everything back. To start over again.

He closed his eyes and forced himself to take a steadying breath. If this were a business deal going sour, he'd figure out a way to reset the discussions, to return to square one. He would offer up an olive branch. He pushed a single button on his BlackBerry, summoning his assistant.

He already had the beginnings of a plan....

The package was leaning against the door when Sloane got back from the library. She had forced herself to get out of the apartment, to take a break from the jumble of hope and confusion that she felt every time she glanced at Ethan's business card. The last time she had acted rashly where he was concerned; now, she was determined to *think,* to make decisions with her brain, instead of with her heart.

That was the plan she'd made as she had stared at the library's public access terminal, resisting the urge to call up articles about Ethan, his company, his philanthropic efforts. His hard-partying ways.

As much as she wanted to tell Ethan everything she was thinking, everything she was feeling, she needed to slow things down. Think things through. She needed to remember that she wasn't making decisions just for herself anymore. There was the baby to think about. There was a reason—the *best* reason—not to be impulsive.

She had to be certain that Ethan was truly more than the socializing playboy she had read about in the paper. She had to know that he had shared more with her than he had with the other women whose names were tied to his in the newspaper. She had to force herself to look past her—admit it!—infatuation, her utter physical attraction to him.

Returning home, she spotted the envelope immediately. She recognized the Hartwell Genetics logo on the address label. Her heart started pounding, but she forced herself to unlock her front door, to pour herself a drink of water from the pitcher in the refrigerator and sit down at the kitchen table. She thought about returning the envelope unopened. She could just write "return to sender" and drop it in the mailbox, couldn't she?

Except that he hadn't sent it through the mail. There wasn't a postmark. He'd had it hand-delivered.

Taking a fortifying breath, she slid her fingers beneath the flap.

"Sloane," the note said. Even though she'd never seen his writing before, she could picture his fingers curled around a pen, slashing out the letters on the heavy white paper. "Give me another chance? E." A ticket was nestled inside the folds of paper.

Swan Lake, the Bolshoi Ballet, opening gala for the dance season at the Kennedy Center. Friday night.

She sank back in the hard chair. What was she getting herself into?

But that wasn't really the question, was it? The question was what *had* she gotten herself into? Two and a half months before, when she'd given in to the magnetic power of the man she'd met at the Eastern, when she'd let herself be drawn into the thrumming, driving force that had risen between them like a river overflowing its banks.

She laid her hand across her belly, across the child that grew inside her.

Sure, she could tell him that she had other plans for Friday night. She could send back the ticket. After all, she was healthy and happy, and she already loved her baby with a sharp fierceness.

But what, exactly, was she going to do, long-term? How was she going to raise this child?

Marry me.

Independence was important to her. It was the one thing that she had always carried with her, the one certainty she had clung to, no matter what had happened in her turbulent childhood, in her confused adolescence. She had built a life for herself, built a dream. Self-reliance had made her the woman that she was today.

Marry me.

She'd scoured job sites every day since leaving the foundation, but there weren't a lot of paying opportunities for psychologists focusing on art therapy for foster kids. That was why she'd ended up at AFAA as a project coordinator in the first place. How much longer would it take for her to find something? How much longer would her meager savings hold out?

Even if she spent the five hundred dollars that he'd left, even if she accepted the money as a gift and not an insult.

Marry me.

He couldn't mean it. He had to have spoken out of surprise, the shock at discovering he was going to be a father. Shock. But why *hadn't* Sloane told him? What had she been proving to herself? To him? That she didn't need him? That she didn't need anyone? Once again, she saw the earnest look in his eyes as he proposed to her, his solemn hazel gaze as he turned his own life upside down. He had not hesitated an instant. He had reached out to her with all his strength, all the certainty that had sparked off him at the Eastern during that fateful night. She could learn to depend on that strength. She could learn to bask in it.

Marry me.

She was crazy to even consider it. Crazier than he'd been to offer. But what better option did she have for her baby? How else could she give her child the comfort, stability and security it deserved?

She stared at the gleaming ticket. What could it hurt, going to the ballet? What did she have to lose?

Her stomach growled as she read Ethan's note again. For the first time in days, she was actually hungry. A burger with cheese and bacon sounded wonderful. And for once, she didn't have to worry about whether she could afford an extra large order of fries.

* * *

Ethan forbade himself to check the time once again. Either she would show up or she wouldn't, and staring at his watch wasn't going to change anything.

The musicians were warming up in the orchestra pit. Violins chased each other in discordant flurries. Horns blared repeated trills of notes. Ethan tapped his program against the arm of his chair, wishing that the theater box was large enough for him to pace.

Opting for the best alternative under the circumstances, he stood. He shot his cuffs and glanced at his wrist again, before he remembered that he wasn't going to check the time.

And then the door to the box opened. For one moment, he could only see the dark shadows of the antechamber. Then, a tentative hand reached out, creamy flesh with perfect crimson nails that sent a reflexive shiver down his spine. Sloane followed the promise of that hand, gliding into the light, a dizzying contrast of sophisticated innocence, of steely vulnerability, all enfolded in a demure, floor-length cobalt gown.

He murmured her name, unable to manage more.

She glanced at the half-dozen chairs arrayed in the box, and the shadow of a frown darted across her lips. "Who else is coming?"

"No one," he said. "I wanted to make sure we had some privacy. The box is ours for tonight."

She blushed and looked away from him, obviously nervous. That surprised him. She'd chosen to come here, to accept his peace offering. And she certainly knew what he was capable of, what they were capable of together. He could recall perfectly how she had responded to his touch, how she had trembled when he traced the line of her collarbone with the tip of his tongue. He could remember the instant that she shifted her hips beneath him, that she matched her thighs to his. He could see the arch of her throat as her breathing quickened, as he guided them closer to the edge of their first delicious peak.

And yet there was more to discover with this woman. More to learn about her. About him *with* her. That notion was strangely arousing. Hoping to put her at ease, he said, "I'm glad you're here."

And he was.

Her hair was piled on top of her head in a simple twist, held in place by some invisible woman's magic. The sleek lines made the column of her neck impossibly long. Impossibly vulnerable. His fingers itched to follow the path of the chaste fabric V across her chest. Instead, he settled for gesturing toward her chair, offering her the best seat in the box.

As she stepped forward, he saw that the modest front of her dress lied. The back was cut low, swooping to bare the twin wings of her shoulder blades, the polished marble of her spine. Awareness of that body, of that perfect flesh, shot through him like an electric wire. She took her seat gracefully, apparently unaware of the havoc she was wreaking inside him, the sudden blow she had dealt his composure.

Sloane had known that Ethan would be in a tuxedo. Nevertheless, the formal suit tugged at her memories, catapulted her back to that night at the Eastern. All too easily, she could see his bow tie stripped loose at his throat. She could picture the tiny onyx studs sprung open down his chest, his cuff links freed to reveal the tight muscles of his forearms.

With perfect recall, she could see those satin-striped trousers pooled on the floor, as if he'd just shed them.

But that wasn't what this night was about. That wasn't why she'd agreed to meet Ethan Hartwell here, at the Kennedy Center. She needed to remember her focus. She needed to remember her goal. She needed to remember that her baby deserved medical care and protection, safety and security, things that she could not afford to provide.

Sloane was grateful she'd taken the time to pin up her hair and paint her nails. And she was thrilled that she could still fit into the improbably perfect dress that she'd found years before, at Goodwill, in Chicago.

She'd never been to the Kennedy Center before, had only seen it on television. The rich crimson of the carpet made her feel like a princess. The gold accents on the light fixtures picked out the blond in Ethan's hair, highlighting the unruly strands that made him look like a slightly naughty boy. She blinked, and in the darkness behind her eyelids, she pictured him balanced over her, nothing at all like a boy, supporting himself on his wiry fingers as he whispered her name.

Sudden longing clutched at her belly. Fortunately, the lights dimmed at that very moment, and she was spared the need to say something, to explain. Instead, she filled her lungs with cool, calming air. She leaned back in her chair as the music began to play. She ordered herself to forget about the man who sat beside her, the monumental force that radiated awareness at her side.

The curtain rose.

The music and the dance carried her away, transformed her. She ached with longing as Prince Siegfried rebelled against his forced marriage, as he fell in love with his forbidden princess. She laughed as the swans frolicked, boastfully completing their duets and trios.

She shivered as the evil Odile appeared, as the lovers' eternal happiness was threatened.

And when it was over, when the curtain fell, Sloane leaped to her feet. The audience joined her, roaring its approval, calling for the dancers again and again. A giant spotlight flooded the center of the stage, and the main dancers stepped out from behind the curtain, sinking into graceful bows, collapsing into flawless curtsies.

"Ethan," she said, when the house lights finally came up. "That was incredible!"

She was incredible.

Ethan had stood with the rest of the audience, and he'd added his applause for the dancers. The entire time, though, he was watching Sloane. His gaze had settled on her waist. There was no sign yet of the child that she carried. *His* child.

He wanted that baby to be healthy. He *needed* it to be healthy.

He brushed his fingers against his breast pocket, reassuring himself that the velvet box was still safely hidden away. He could follow through on this. He *had* to follow through. The stakes had gone up exponentially back in Sloane's grimy little apartment. This was no longer a sparring match with his grandmother. This was something more. So much more.

Sloane was biting her lip as she turned her back on the now-curtained stage. He was startled to see tear tracks on her cheeks, silver trails that glistened in the theater's golden light.

He closed the distance between them, settling a hand just beneath her elbow. "What's wrong?"

Sloane raised her hand to her cheek and was somehow surprised when her fingers came away wet. "I—"

she started to say, but her emotions were still perilously close to the surface.

Ethan produced a flawless handkerchief from his pocket, scarcely taking a moment to shake it out before he handed it to her. She smiled her thanks, not ready to trust words yet, and she dabbed the cloth beneath her eyes, careful not to touch her mascara. Thank heavens she'd splurged on the waterproof stuff.

Her emotions had been jangled ever since that night at the Eastern. She slammed her mind closed to the memories that cascaded over her, to the image of sheets as white as the handkerchief she now clutched.

"I thought that we could head up to the roof terrace," Ethan said, smoothly filling the silence, as if she'd been conversing like a normal human being. "The breeze is always nice in June."

He waited until she nodded, and then he gestured to the door, settling one hand against the small of her back. She could feel the heat of his touch through her dress. Somehow, his presence calmed her, gave her strength.

The audience had dispersed, eager to find their way to the garage, to their cars, to their homes. Ethan, though, led her to a deserted bank of elevators. He punched the call button with authority, as if he owned the place. The doors opened immediately, and Sloane imagined that the car had been waiting just for them.

Upstairs, in the rooftop lounge, a kaleidoscope of people spun through a huge white gallery. Waiters hovered with trays of champagne and miniature desserts, ready with a constant supply of napkins. The gala, Sloane remembered belatedly. These people must be donors to the Kennedy Center, to the Bolshoi dance company. Wealthy donors, like the ones who had been so offended by her going off with Ethan after the AFAA auction.

Clearly unaware of her flash of guilty memory, Ethan guided her through the crowd with silent determination. A handful of men glanced at them, nodding like solemn butlers. A half-dozen women were more aggressive, flocking toward Ethan like exotic butterflies, turning from chattering conversation to raise glasses of sparkling wine, to smile open invitations.

One dared to separate herself from the crowd, slinking forward in a crimson dress that looked like woven sin. "Ethan," she cooed, stepping directly in front of him and spreading her talons across his chest. "You promised that you'd call after Chase's party last week. You still owe me dessert." She licked her pouty lips, making it clear exactly what she intended to eat.

Sloane's fingers tightened around the handkerchief she still held. Here it was. The moment when everything changed. The moment when Ethan went back to his playboy ways, to the behavior that made him the darling of every gossip columnist this side of the Rockies.

Ethan, though, merely slid his hand around Sloane's waist, pulling her close in a way that left no doubt about his intent. "I'm sorry, Elaine," he said. "I've been busy."

The woman's face twisted from seduction to cold anger. "Ellen," she spat. "My name is Ellen."

Ethan shrugged, using the motion to pull Sloane even closer. "Ellen," he repeated, as if he were accepting some minor point of clarification in a business meeting. The woman spluttered, obviously lost for words, and then Ethan nodded. "Good evening," he said, concluding the conversation with perfect courtesy.

Three steps farther on, a photographer materialized

from nowhere. "Mr. Hartwell," he said. "Something for the *Washington Banner?*"

"No comment," Ethan snarled, striding forward with a long enough gait that Sloane had to skip three short steps to catch up.

The photographer looked surprised, then angry. He scurried in front of them and took a half-dozen photos, letting his flash spawn a dizzying array of bright white spots. Ethan stepped forward, his shoulders squaring, but the photographer hopped off before the situation could escalate.

Sloane grabbed for Ethan's arm, as much for support while her vision cleared as to calm him down. No one else approached them before they reached the twin glass doors that led to the outdoor terrace. "Something to drink?" he asked, before they could escape.

Sloane nodded.

"Go ahead, then. I'll be out in a moment." He stalked toward the bar before she could change her mind, before she could beg him to stay beside her.

She stepped onto the terrace alone. The June night was balmy, and she stared at the moonlit landscape. This was the beautiful Washington, the vibrant one. Her basement apartment, with its dim light and clunky TV, was a lifetime away from this grace and elegance. She relaxed a bit, watching the golden lights of a boat moving silently up the Potomac River, toward the wealthy enclave of Georgetown. Everything was golden here— lights and laughter and endless, glowing potential.

The doors opened behind her, releasing a clamor from the party within. Sloane tensed at the noise, or at the presence of the man who glided up to her side. Ethan didn't speak as he passed her a glass, a champagne flute. She caught a hint of lime amid the tiny bubbles, and a single sip confirmed that he'd brought her sparkling water. She was grateful that he'd thought of the baby.

He kept a highball glass for himself. His wrist tensed, and he swirled ice cubes in some amber liquor. Scotch, she remembered from the Eastern. The finest single malt the bar could serve. She remembered the smoky echo on his tongue, and her breath caught at the back of her throat.

"Thank you," he said, staring across the water.

"For what?" She was astonished.

"For coming here tonight. For trusting me that much."

She'd trusted him a lot more, back at the Eastern. She'd trusted him the way she'd never trusted another man. But in the past three days, as she'd thought about his offer, about their future, she'd realized that she needed to give him more than just her body. As crazy as it seemed, she needed to give him her future. The future of their child.

She held her glass against the pulse point in her right wrist. She wished that she had the courage to reach for his drink, for the ice cubes that she longed to sacrifice against the fever he lit inside her blood. She wasn't going to acknowledge that heat. She couldn't. This conversation wasn't about that sort of satisfaction.

So far, so good, Ethan thought.

She wasn't running away from him. She hadn't been frightened off by that bird-brained idiot, Elaine.

And Ethan hadn't wasted too much time back inside. Stepping away from the bar, he'd been cornered by Zach Crosby, who had raised an eyebrow at Ethan's two glasses. "You work fast, my man. Who's tonight's lucky lady?"

"Who's asking? My best friend? Or my grandmother's attorney?"

A frown had clouded Zach's face. "You know I can't talk to you about that. I *can* tell you that I advised her against drawing up the papers, though. No hard feelings?"

Ethan had sighed. Zach had been placed in an impossible position. Margaret Hartwell was his biggest client, by far. Besides, the men's friendship had survived a lot worse, from elementary school escapades to college pranks. "No hard feelings," he'd said grudgingly.

"So you'll introduce me to the woman of the hour? Give me a chance to warn her about you?"

"Absolutely not." Ethan had smiled, but he'd continued walking toward the door, toward the balcony where Sloane waited.

"Hey!" Zach had called after him. "What about the silent auction?"

Damn. Zach was in charge of the ballet fundraiser. Ethan had already promised to place a bid, to make a sizable donation. "Put me down for something. You know my limit."

Zach had laughed, and Ethan had escaped to the terrace.

Now, he watched Sloane sip from her champagne flute. Her throat barely rippled as she swallowed. He wanted to trace the liquid with his tongue, to edge aside the dark V that shielded her breasts.

She felt his attention on her. She'd never had any man so aware of her, so focused on her every move. It made her feel…treasured. Protected. Bold enough to say, "What's this all about, Ethan?"

"What do you mean?" A caged wariness flashed into his hazel eyes.

She set her champagne flute on the ground at her feet, as if she could distance herself from the perfect night, from the old dreams that had spun awake as the dancers twirled upon the stage. "I mean, the view is beautiful, and the ballet was gorgeous, and I really appreciate your bringing me here." She let the brightness fade from her voice. "But why do you want to marry me? You're not exactly the type to settle down. We spent *one night* together."

"It was a damned good night," he growled.

The heat behind his words kindled a slow fire inside her, and she had to concentrate to say, "I've read about you, Ethan, over and over again, in all the papers. You've had nights like that before. You've been with lots of other women, but I've never heard of you proposing to one of them."

The simple truth was that not one of those other women had been anything like Sloane. Ethan had thought long and hard since leaving her apartment three days before. *Something* had broken through his usual reserve to make him say those terrifying two words. *Something* had driven him to speak out. *Marry me.*

He'd tried to shrug it off, to tell himself that he was merely overreacting to his grandmother's absurd demand. His grandmother was being manipulative. She was pushing his buttons. She was overstepping her bounds.

But he had a lifetime of practice ignoring his grandmother.

Besides, only a fool would completely ignore a trusted confidante. And as infuriating as Grandmother could be, she *had* raised him. She knew him better than any person in the entire world, better even than Zach. Ethan had seen the honest concern on his grandmother's face; he had recognized the heartsick worry that had softened her to tears when she spoke her mind about his womanizing. If she truly believed that his spending mind-less time with a shifting parade of women made him a weaker businessman—a lesser man—then he had to give some credence to what she said. He had to accept the business argument.

And who better to settle down with than the woman who stood beside him? Sloane was *real*. She had true dreams, actual goals. If he closed his eyes, he could still feel her nestled beside him in bed at the Eastern, her body as spent as his but her mind still restless, still in-tent on sharing, on telling him what she wanted to build, how she wanted to make the world a better place.

Not one of them has been like you. He longed to em-phasize his words with a touch. He could see the vulner-able curve of Sloane's jaw. Just trace it with a finger... turn her toward him, tilt her head, slant her lips beneath his own.

But he couldn't touch her now. This had to be about more than simply the lust of his body for hers.

He forced himself to swallow a raw mouthful of Scotch, to substitute one heat with another.

Sloane filled the silence that had stretched out for far too long, making herself say the painful words, the diffi-cult admission that she'd thought about for three straight days. "We had a single night, Ethan. I'm no different than those other women are. I'm not going to hold you to some promise that you made on the spur of the mo-ment. I'm not going to use our baby to force you to do anything you don't really want to do." There. She'd said it. She'd voiced her greatest fear. Whatever Ethan said now, she would know that she had been true to herself. True to her child.

As if in answer, he set his glass next to hers before reaching inside the pocket of his jacket. In the darkness of the terrace, it took a moment to decipher what he took out. The black velvet nearly disappeared into the night. He offered it to her on his open palm, his fingers extended as if he were trying to gentle a wild animal.

She plucked the box from his hand before she was fully aware of what it was. The hinge was stiff; one curious touch threw the box open to the moonlight and the stars. She caught her breath as she saw the most stunning diamond ring she'd ever imagined. An emerald cut, perfect in its simplicity. A platinum band. Two carats, at least.

"Ethan," she breathed, half-afraid that the ring would disappear as she broke its magic spell.

When he'd blurted out his proposal on Tuesday, she hadn't really believed him. She couldn't. Things like that didn't happen to her, had *never* happened to her.

But a diamond ring was different. A diamond ring, offered to her here under the stars, meant that he'd thought this whole thing through. He meant it.

If she passed the paternity test, a nasty voice whispered at the back of her mind. But of course she would pass it. And he'd be a fool to take her word that the baby was his, without medical proof. She'd already seen the swarm of women waiting for his attention back there in the gallery. He had to protect himself.

The negative thought, though, fed her other insecurities. How could she be certain that he would stay with her? Sure, he said that she was different, that the night they'd shared was special. And, in a way, it was. It had resulted in a child. But the baby was one truth, placed in a balance against all the other truths she had learned, all the articles she'd forced herself to read. Ethan Hartwell was not the kind of man who settled down. He wasn't the kind of man who married.

But he was the kind of man who could pay for visits to an obstetrician. And for a pediatrician, after that. And for all the other things that Sloane desired for her baby. For Ethan's baby. For their child together.

She looked down at the stunning engagement ring. Her hands started to shake, hard enough that she was afraid she would drop the velvet box. With a comforting smile, Ethan rescued the ring from its midnight bed. He snapped the box closed, then made it disappear in the pocket of his trousers. His burning fingers grasped hers, steadying her, pouring some iron behind her trembling knees. Carefully, like a surgeon performing a delicate operation, he slid the band onto the ring finger of her left hand.

It fit perfectly. The metal melted into her flesh, as if it had always been a piece of her. The diamond collected all the light in the heavens above, casting it back at her dazed eyes in a thousand tiny flashes.

Ethan thought that the ring looked even better on her hand than he had imagined when he'd selected it at the jewelers. Watching the wonder spread across her face, the wash of joy that echoed the pure physical bliss they'd shared at the Eastern, Ethan folded his hands around hers. She blinked as he covered the brilliance of the ring, almost as if he were breaking some spell. He stepped closer to her, tucking her captured hand against the pleated front of his shirt. He felt the flutter of her pleasure through his palm, measured the solid drumbeat of his own heart through her flesh.

"Sloane Davenport," he said, his voice a husky whisper. "Will you be my wife?"

This time her tears remained unshed, glistening in the night. "Yes," she whispered. "Yes, I will."

He folded his arms around her. Her bare back seared

through his sleeves. He had to hold her, had to feel her, had to crush her against the entire length of his body, so that he could truly believe that this was happening, that she was real. His lips found hers, and he drank deeply, swallowing her incredulous laughter as his tongue demanded more. He closed his teeth against her lower lip with a surge of passion, barely heeding the internal rein that reminded him to be careful, to protect her, to spare the woman who bore his child.

"Ethan," she gasped, finally tearing away from the pressure of his kiss. Her lips felt bruised, swollen, pulsing with the hot blood that he had sucked into them. For a dozen heartbeats, he fought to reclaim her mouth, pressed himself into her, seeking to slake his apparently never-ending thirst.

She couldn't let him, though. She couldn't let herself forget her decision, the why and the wherefore of it. She had to be strong, and true to her baby. "Ethan," she said again, finally managing to lay her palm along his jaw. Her left palm. With the diamond ring winking beside his midnight stubble. "I'll marry you, but there's one condition."

"Yes," he said immediately, the single word a promise and a plea.

She bit back a smile. "No." She shook her head. "You need to listen to me. You need to decide."

His fingers clenched on her hips, but she held his gaze steadily. She had to say this. Had to make sure that her heart knew precisely what she was doing and why she was doing it. She had to make everything absolutely clear.

If she had learned nothing else working on the Hope Project, she had learned this: Children deserved to be with families that loved them. Families that functioned healthily, without parental angst, without adult trials and tribulations constantly undermining stability. All of the art projects in the world could never create what every baby should have from birth: a stable, loving home.

And Sloane couldn't think of anything more likely to turn a relationship upside down than sex. Sex with Ethan had been wonderful, more fulfilling than she'd ever dreamed. But it had made her lose sight of her goals. Sleeping with Ethan had cost her a job. She wasn't going to let a physical relationship take away more—not when her child was at risk.

"If I marry you, Ethan, it can't be because of what happened at the Eastern. It can't be because of…this." She looked down, managing to convey both their bodies, the crumpled clothes between them. "It can't be about… about sex. I won't go to bed with you until after we're married. We both need that break. That separation. We both need to be certain that we're getting married for the right reason—for our baby."

He understood what she was doing. Despite her finding the courage to meet him tonight, she was unnerved by their passion, by the animal need that had drawn them together, that hummed between them, even now, like the echo of a gong.

But that was why he'd been drawn to her in the first place, wasn't it? The freshness of her innocence. The honesty that she'd brought to bed with her. That was what had intrigued him, made him realize that she was different from every other woman he'd ever had. It had been a pure bonus to discover that there was more to Sloane than a beautiful face, a gorgeous body. Her passion for her work had been like a decadent dessert after a sating meal—stunning because it was unnecessary. Unexpected.

If only Sloane still wanted *him,* after she learned the truth about his Hartwell genes. If only she kept her promise to marry him after the fourteenth week, after the testing that would disclose whether Ethan was as cursed as his own parents had been, twice. He couldn't let himself think about that, though. Couldn't think about losing Sloane.

Better to play the role she was expecting. Better to pretend that he knew there would always be a happy ending. Better to give in to the passion that he could barely restrain when she was anywhere near.

He raised her wrist to his mouth. His lips hovered above her trembling pulse, barely touching her throbbing flesh. He heard the moan that she caught at the back of her throat, and then he darted out his tongue to taste her. He clamped his fingers around her arm when she jumped away in surprise, and he used the motion to pull her close to his chest.

"You'll change your mind," he said. "After a few weeks? Months? How long do you think it will take to plan a wedding?" He leaned down and whispered against her lips, "I promise. You *will* change your mind."

She shook her head, her eyes gone round. "I won't," she whispered. "I can't."

"You will," he said. "You already have. And when you admit that, you'll have to tell me. You'll have to ask for what you truly want."

She shook her head, her throat working, but no words rose to the surface.

He pulled back, settling for planting one last kiss in the palm of her hand. "Remember this," he said. "Remember now. You will."

Chapter Three

When Sloane awoke, her bedroom was dark, even though the clock said 9:27 a.m. She sighed and rolled onto her back. It must be raining outside. She usually got *some* glimmer of light from the front room.

She flicked on the bedside lamp, and her gaze was snagged by the ring on her finger. Collapsing against her pillow, she turned her wrist in the wan yellow light. It was real, then. Not some fevered dream.

Ethan had proposed to her. And she had accepted.

It had seemed like magic the night before, edged in fog, lost in impossibility. Following Ethan's smooth certainty that she would keep their relationship physical, that she would yield to the powerful temptation he provided every time he was within a hundred yards, Sloane had insisted on returning home alone. She'd needed to make that point. Needed to prove something to him. To herself.

With a tolerant smile, Ethan had acquiesced, instructing his driver to ferry her through the city streets. She supposed that he'd taken a cab to his own home. Sloane had walked from the dark Town Car to her front door, certain that she was going to wake up at any moment, positive that she was going to discover this was all some strange dream. But the ring was still on her finger, even in the gloomy light of a rainy summer morning. She was engaged to be married.

Sloane Hartwell.

Mrs. Ethan Hartwell.

She tested the names against the brittle edge of her emotions. Getting engaged was supposed to be one of the highlights of her life. She was supposed to call her mother, her girlfriends. Well, no mother to call, that was for sure. And no real girlfriends, either. Unless she wanted to count the librarian who helped out with the public access computers. As a child, she had never brought friends home to her foster families; life had been too chaotic. As an adult, she had been focused on juggling college and work, on fighting for the Hope Project to become a reality. While Sloane had plenty of acquaintances, she was poorer than she liked to admit when it came to true friends.

She sighed and settled her ringed hand on her belly. "Well, little one. We'll just have to be happy for each other, won't we?"

As if in answer, her stomach rumbled, reminding Sloane that she'd been too nervous to eat dinner the night before. She threw her feet over the side of her bed and tugged on her ratty terry-cloth bathrobe. The fabric had rubbed completely bare across the elbows, but there was never anyone around to notice, so she hadn't bothered to replace it.

Stumbling into the kitchen, Sloane filled the teakettle and put it on the stove. It took three tries before the burner lit; she'd have to call her landlord to have him fix the silly thing. Again. She glanced at the minute patch of window left visible beside the hulking air conditioner. She'd been right—it *was* raining, the steady tropical downpour that often hit D.C. in the summer.

As she waited for the water to boil, she heard a rustle outside her front door. Her landlord's cat had probably gotten trapped in the alcove, driven to seek a dry corner in the midst of the torrential rain. The sweet calico had sought refuge from summer storms before. Sloane could let her nap on the couch until the storm passed. Sloane braced herself to get her feet wet as she completed Operation Cat Rescue.

"Sloane!"

"Ms. Davenport!"

"Sloane Davenport!"

The alcove was filled with people, with the flash of cameras, with a half-dozen microphones. Sloane stared at them, slack jawed. Where had they come from? And what could they possibly want with her?

One voice soared above the others, as harsh as pumice. "Sloane, show us your ring! Tell us how you caught the most eligible guy in town!"

Reflexively, she clutched at her robe, pulling it across her belly. Even as she glanced down, frantic to make sure that she was covered, that no one could see her faded pink nightgown, she realized that she might be sending some sort of signal to the press, telegraphing the presence of the baby. She dropped the terry, as if it had burned her fingers.

All the while, cameras continued to flash, and the crowd jostled for position on the three narrow steps.

Sloane's throat started to close; she couldn't draw a full breath. She didn't want these people here, didn't want them anywhere near her.

A terrific flash of lightning, brighter even than the cameras in her face, made her squeeze her eyes closed. Instinct made her hunch her shoulders close to her ears, waiting for the inevitable boom of thunder. When it came, it drowned out the reporters' chatter. All of a sudden, she remembered the way Ethan had handled the photographer the night before. She took a deep breath, determined to make her voice as steely as possible. "No comment," she said.

She closed the door before anyone could protest, before someone could tell her that *she* didn't have the right to refuse to talk. The teakettle chose that moment to reach its boiling point, the shriek of its whistle sounding like a train racing toward her. She rescued the kettle before it could deafen her permanently, setting it onto a cold burner before she crept back to the front door.

Leaning against the wooden panels, she could hear the horde shifting outside. They called her name a half-dozen times, as if she might change her mind and come back out to play. There was only one thing to do. It took her a couple of minutes to find Ethan's business card. She had stashed it in the folder with her working papers for the Hope Project. Her fingers were trembling by the time she punched in the ten digits.

"Ethan Hartwell's office," a woman answered on the first ring.

Sloane gritted her teeth. Given the fact that it was a Saturday morning, she had hoped Ethan might answer his own phone. Feeling absurd, she said, "This is Sloane Davenport, calling for Mr. Hartwell." What sort of woman called her fiancé Mr. Anything?

"I'll see if Mr. Hartwell is in his office." The secretary didn't give the faintest hint of recognizing her name. Classical music filled the silence, and Sloane fought the urge to hang up.

"Sloane." Ethan's voice was warm as honey. "Good morning." He managed to make the standard greeting sound seductive.

That unspoken promise in his tone shattered her taut emotions. "Ethan!" His name turned into a sob.

"What's wrong?" His demand was immediate. "Sloane, are you all right? Is it the baby?"

"No," she gasped, shocked into realizing what a fright she was giving him. "No, I'm sorry. I…it's just the people. Paparazzi. They're outside. I heard them out there, thought it was my landlord's cat. I shouldn't have opened the door. They won't leave me alone!"

Ethan swore, the words low and fluid and unerringly precise.

"I don't know how they found out about us," Sloane cried. "I don't know what I did!"

Even as anger flashed crimson behind Ethan's eyes, he consciously gentled his voice. "You didn't do anything, Sloane. This isn't your fault."

"But how…" She trailed off, and he could hear her gasping for a full breath, struggling to regain control.

"This isn't your fault," he repeated. But he knew whose fault it was. He knew that his driver last night was new, had only been hired two weeks before. The man had been cleared by Hartwell Genetics's security team, and he'd possessed all the required credentials, up to and including U.S. Marines evasive driving training. But that didn't mean the guy was above selling information—especially valuable gossip, like a Hartwell date going home with a diamond ring on her left hand.

Ethan wondered how much the driver had gotten from the rabid press corps. Not enough. The man would never work in D.C. again.

But none of that mattered. Not now. Not with Sloane sobbing on the other end of the line.

"I'm sorry," he said. "I thought you'd have more time."

"More time?" There. That was more like it. She was already getting herself under control. Just as well—she wasn't going to like the rest of this conversation.

"You saw the photographer at the gala last night. Now that your name is out there, it'll be like blood in the water. The sharks won't back off until they've fed."

"Ethan, why do they care about *me?* I'm no one!"

"You're someone to me," he said. He thought about adding a smooth line, something to make her blush. He was certain that he'd be able to tell that she was flustered, even over the phone. But this wasn't the time. He might as well rip off this Band-Aid. It was going to be the first of many. "I'm sending over a man, Daniel Alton. He's the head of corporate security here."

"Ethan, I don't think that's necessary."

"I do." He wasn't in any mood to listen to arguments. Not when he knew he'd win them all in the long run. "Daniel will canvass your apartment. His assessment will help the movers."

"Movers?" He heard the shock in her voice, but he steeled himself against her protest.

"Pack a suitcase now, whatever you need for the next twenty-four hours. Daniel will bring you to my home this morning. The rest of your belongings will be transferred tomorrow."

Sloane glanced at the telephone handset. He had to

be kidding. Pack an overnight bag and leave her entire life behind? "Ethan, I can't do that."

"Yes," he said. "You can."

She could picture him now, standing behind whatever massive table passed for a desk in his office. He would have taken off his suit jacket when he arrived at work. His stark white sleeves were rolled up, revealing the dusting of golden hair on his forearms.

Forget about his forearms!

Sloane swallowed a strangled noise. She tested her voice inside her head before she spoke, and when she delivered her words they were measured. Even. "I agreed to marry you, Ethan. I didn't agree to let you run my life. And I certainly didn't agree to enter a prison."

She expected him to argue with her. She expected him to thread steel into his voice. She expected him to respond with the utter control, the absolute mastery she'd already seen him exercise in other aspects of his life.

She was unprepared for the catch in his throat as he said, "I know you didn't, Sloane." Quickly, though, his words grew urgent, intense. "I need to keep you safe, though. I want to keep you away from those reporters, from people who will take away your freedom. Our freedom. Trust me on this. Move into my house. Let me protect you. You and the baby."

The baby.

That was the key, wasn't it? If Sloane were alone, she could do whatever she wanted.

But she wasn't making decisions just for herself anymore. She couldn't act blindly. She'd lost that ability when she'd chosen to follow Ethan to his hotel suite, when she'd given in to the fiery compulsion, to the impossible certainty that he was the man she wanted to be with, *needed* to be with.

When she'd said that she would marry him.

"Okay," she said.

Ethan exhaled slowly, all of a sudden aware that he'd been holding his breath. "Thank you, Sloane." He shuddered and shifted back to professional mode. "Daniel will be there in an hour. He'll call from his cell when he's outside your door."

By the time Ethan hung up the phone, he was already reviewing everything that needed to be done. One call to Daniel, dispatching him to Sloane's apartment. Another call to the house, telling James to prepare the guest suite. He paused, then, his fingers poised over the speed-dial button, as he weighed making a third call.

By now, Grandmother had to know that Sloane existed. There was certainly some notice on the newspaper gossip page, probably a picture from that obnoxious photographer at the gala. But Grandmother was used to reading about his liaisons, used to discounting them. She wouldn't believe that Ethan had actually chosen a wife until he told her, himself. And she would never imagine that her long-awaited great-grandchild was truly on the way.

Sloane had enough on her plate for now, without meeting the Hartwell matriarch. Ethan *could* give his fiancée a reprieve, and so he would. Just like with the genetic testing.

Grandmother might be unhappy when she learned the truth. But Sloane's happiness was far more important to Ethan now. Grandmother would just have to wait.

Sloane knew she should be grateful. Precisely as Ethan had described, Daniel retrieved her from her apartment, lifting her suitcase with one hand, firmly grasping her elbow with the other. He led her past the soaking-wet reporters, growling the "no comment" that she'd already come to understand was now her standard way of life. He settled her in the back of yet another Town Car, taking the driver's seat himself.

James greeted her at the house. Sloane had to smile. The older man looked like somebody's uncle. He wore neat khakis and a polo shirt that barely managed to cover his potbelly. He took Sloane's bag from Daniel, nodding an amiable dismissal, and then he ushered her into the kitchen. A cup of chamomile tea and a fresh-baked cinnamon roll later, Sloane was almost ready to believe that being transplanted to Ethan's home was a good thing.

She had the better part of the day to think about it, and the evening besides. Ethan sent a message through James. Some production matter had come up at the Swiss plant, and he was going to be late coming home.

A production matter. On a Saturday.

Sloane shivered in the aggressive air conditioning.

What was she getting into? Who was this man she had agreed to marry? A workaholic who spent his entire life at the office? She needed better for their baby. She would fight for more.

James showed Sloane into the library. He helped her log on to a laptop computer kept for the convenience of guests. She sighed at the springy touch of the keyboard, so unlike the brick that she'd rescued from her own apartment. She was eager to get back to work on the Hope Project. But tomorrow would be soon enough. She had even more important work to do. She needed to organize her thoughts.

Taking a deep breath, she clicked on the button that

launched a word processor. Half an hour later, she was still staring at an empty document. What, exactly, did she want from Ethan? What did she expect to get out of their marriage? And why was she so afraid to commit anything to a silly computer file?

Ethan Hartwell, she finally typed across the top of the screen. To delay a little more, she retyped his name, in all capitals. She made the font bold, and she underscored the two words, hitting the enter key twice to place the cursor at the beginning of a new line.

Unable to delay further, she typed a new word. *Trust.* She needed to trust Ethan. Needed to believe that he would always be there for her and the baby, that his days of playboy escapades were over forever.

Respect, she added. She needed Ethan to respect her. To appreciate what was important to her—the Hope Project, for example—even if he never fully embraced it himself.

Friendship, she typed. She stared at the cursor blinking after the word. What did she mean by friendship? She didn't have enough practice to understand the concept herself. Shaking her head, she backspaced carefully.

Partnership, she wrote instead. She and Ethan needed to be equals. They needed to talk, to share, to accept each other on level ground.

Trust. Respect. Partnership.

That sounded more like a formula for a business arrangement than for a marriage. But what else could she type? "True love"? How could she demand that? How could Ethan promise it? True love was something that either happened or it didn't; it couldn't be subject to negotiation.

Sloane sighed, and then she typed something else, at

the bottom of her list. A date—a deadline for their wedding. The baby was due at the end of December. Add three months to get back in shape. Another three months to actually plan the wedding. June 1 of next year. That was the earliest that they could get married, the first possible date that made any sense at all.

Sloane leaned back against her rich leather chair. Here it was: a foundation for her entire relationship with Ethan. She glanced at the broad desk situated beneath the mullioned windows. A wireless printer waited to do her bidding. A flurry of keystrokes, and she had a crisp sheet of paper in hand. She read over her words one last time before she folded the document into thirds and tucked it into her purse.

Just as she was beginning to get hungry, James appeared with a chicken sandwich on a tray. He seemed to understand that Sloane needed time alone though, time to process the changes in her life. He left her in the mahogany-and-leather library until nearly sunset, when he carried in another tray, this one sporting a lightly dressed shrimp salad. "Sloane," he said, interrupting her as she checked her email. "I'll be heading home for the evening."

"Home?"

He gestured out the window, across the spacious yard. "I live in the carriage house, out back."

"I thought—" She'd just assumed that James lived in the house. He clearly was responsible for every aspect of the mansion's smooth operation. Sloane had already come to count on his presence. She'd even considered that James would be a sort of chaperone as she got used to living with the man she was going to marry.

"This works out better for everyone," he said, with a twinkle in his eye. "A little privacy can go a long way.

Every phone in the main building has a direct line to the carriage house. Just press zero if you need me, and it will ring out there."

Sloane nodded, but she couldn't imagine having a property large enough to sport a carriage house. And she certainly couldn't imagine having a—what? A butler? A housekeeper? A *friend?*—at her beck and call. "Thank you," she said a little belatedly. "I appreciate everything you've done for me."

"It's not often that we have such a lovely visitor in the guest suite." James winked and left her to her own devices.

Lovely visitor. Ha. Ethan Hartwell had plenty of lovely visitors. Sloane wasn't about to forget that.

But James had no doubt chosen his words carefully. *In the guest suite* he'd said. Ethan's usual "lovely visitors" must not stay in the suite. Ethan probably sent them home in the dark of night, before they could get any ideas about settling in for a long stay.

Sloane closed her eyes, letting her memories catapult her back to the terrace at the Kennedy Center. She remembered the shock of electricity that had jolted through her as Ethan kissed her palm, the liquid heat that had tempted her to change her mind then and there, to dismiss the promise that he had just made, the promise to curb the need that shimmered between them like a physical thing.

No. She was right to insist on that restraint. She had to prove to Ethan that there was something more between them, something deeper than the pure physical attraction that sparked whenever they were in the same room. She needed to be certain—for herself, and for the baby.

Sloane closed the laptop, making sure that it was

firmly latched. She'd grab a book and head upstairs to her room. There was no telling when Ethan was coming home, and she certainly wasn't going to wait up for him like an overeager puppy. Or a mistress. Heading over to the shelves that she'd studied so many times that day, she picked up *Cannery Row.* She'd never read the Steinbeck classic, and it looked light. Enjoyable.

James had left a trail of lights on, guiding her from the library to her suite of rooms. Stepping over the threshold, she took a deep breath, filling her lungs with the scent of roses. A riot of three-dozen long-stemmed beauties overflowed a cut-crystal vase on the dresser. White, pink, yellow and peach. Someone had studiously avoided sending any message with red.

Had Ethan ordered the flowers? Or had James taken care of the detail, just another one of his homey services? Were not-red roses the standing order of the day where "lovely visitors" were concerned?

She could see that James had turned down the sheets on the king-size bed. She half expected to find a mint left on her pillow. Shaking her head, she turned to unpack her suitcase. She'd been lazy all afternoon; she should have hung up her clothes before now. Well, better late than never.

Except that her suitcase was nowhere to be found.

She looked on either side of the bed. Under the massive wooden frame. Behind the bedroom door.

At last, realization dawned on her. She crossed to the large closet that James had indicated when he'd first shown her around the house. Opening the door, she discovered a room that was nearly as large as the entire apartment she'd left behind.

And there, huddling like refugees in a border camp, were her clothes. A quick check of the bathroom confirmed that her drugstore toiletries were displayed on the counter like crown jewels, looking sad amid luxurious towels and gleaming fixtures. Sloane shook her head. This was too much. It was all too much.

After finishing in the bathroom, she sighed deeply as she climbed into the bed. The mattress was twice the size of the beaten-up old bed in her apartment. The peach-and-honey-colored sheets were crisp and cool, even on this muggy June night. A featherweight comforter settled over her body with a whisper.

She lay back on the pillow and forced herself to take a dozen deep breaths. She imagined the picture she would draw if she could fire up her computer, if she could use the Hope Project's specialized software. There'd be a mommy and a daddy and a baby, all standing on Ethan's front lawn, all happy and healthy and together.

The wind picked up outside, and a tree's wooden fingers scraped against her window, shattering the bright image she was painting inside her mind. It was going to be a long, long night.

Ethan paused outside the door of the guest suite. He glanced at his watch. A few minutes past two. Well, no reason that he *should* expect to see a glint of light under the door, was there?

He sighed in frustration. This wasn't the way he'd planned on having Sloane arrive at his home. Oh, it certainly seemed that things had gone smoothly once Daniel had gotten her out of that godforsaken apartment. He hoped that she wasn't going to insist on bringing along any of her furniture; none of it deserved even a brief afterlife in some college dorm room.

James had reported that Sloane had settled in well.

With the nonstop rain, she shouldn't have minded being cooped up in the house. Too much.

But Ethan regretted having spent the entire day at the office. The Swiss production problem should never have taken so long to resolve. At least everything would be back online by Monday morning.

In fact, he'd managed to turn the Zurich fiasco into a good thing. Grandmother had insisted on heading over there to monitor the new quality assurance process for a few days. The quick trip would be a win-win. His grandmother could exercise her iron will over the Swiss plant, and the foreign engineers would learn just how serious Hartwell Genetics was about its demands. At first, Ethan had worried about the strain of travel, but that concern faded after he managed to convince Grandmother to spend a few weeks in her Paris apartment before she came home.

Those would be a few weeks that Ethan could spend getting his own life in order, getting past the all-important genetic testing with Sloane. He carefully hid his true concerns, convincing his grandmother that he only wanted Pierre and Jeanette to pamper her in her luxurious Seventh Arrondissement home. Looking out at the Eiffel Tower, she could get all the rest that she deserved.

Rest. He could use some himself. He should go to bed, get some sleep, wait to see Sloane in the morning. But he couldn't resist opening her door.

The sight inside made him catch his breath.

Sloane had kicked the summer comforter onto the floor where it huddled at the foot of her bed like a lumpy ghost. Her sheets were tangled, nearly tied into knots. Even in the silvery moonlight, he could see that her feet were caught in the twisted mess. Her hair was splayed across her pillow, like seaweed trailing on a beach. Somewhere in her sleep, she must have heard his soft grunt of amazement. She rolled from her side to her back, her arms lashing out in the darkness. "No," she moaned, rubbing at her face. "Please. No."

He stepped into the room before he was consciously aware of moving. As if she could sense his presence, Sloane grew more agitated. Her breath caught in a sob, and she pushed away the confining chains of her sheets. Her fingers snagged in the colorless cotton of her nightgown, and she struggled like a desperate child.

The scent of roses filled the room. He saw the flowers that he'd ordered, faded to gray in the moonlight. He thought he'd been so clever, choosing chaste flowers. He had thought it would be their joke, their secret, a floral memory of the silly, brave promise she'd extracted from him the night before. Now, though, the roses looked like rotten rags and their perfume reminded him of a funeral parlor.

The dead oak tree outside the window swayed in a sudden breeze, scraping its branches against the window. The sound grated like fingers on a chalkboard, and it raised the hairs on the back of his neck. The screech must have penetrated Sloane's nightmare, because she started sobbing in earnest, her words drowned in hopeless, helpless sorrow.

He was beside the bed before he could think.

"Hush," he whispered, settling his palm against her cheek.

She fought like a wild thing, thrashing against the sheets, flinging herself away from him. "Sloane," he murmured, trying to wake her gently, to ease her out of her nightmare. He gathered up the sheets that bound her, shoving them toward the foot of the bed. Her feet were still tangled, and he edged his hands past her thighs, along her calves, fighting to free her ankles. "Sloane," he said again, sitting on the edge of the bed, folding his arms around her, gathering her close to his chest. "I'm here. It's all right. You were having a bad dream."

She shook her head, still dazed, obviously confused. He tightened his grip, pulling her onto his lap. Her head rested on his shoulder; her fingers clutched at the crisp broadcloth of his shirt. "Hush," he said again. "I'm here. You're fine."

The oak fingers scraped against the window again, and she tensed in his arms. He fought the urge to swear out loud. The damned tree had been struck by lightning the summer before. James had hoped that it would recover, but Ethan would have it cut down in the morning.

"It's just a tree," he said. "Just a dream." He started rocking her, gently easing his hand down the trembling plane of her back. He was relieved when her sobs quieted, when her breathing started to slow.

Sloane forced her fingers to loosen their death grip on Ethan's shirt. What had she been thinking? How had she gotten so lost inside her dream? Even now, the nightmare was fading; she could scarcely remember the horror that she'd been fighting. She was awake enough to feel foolish, absolutely idiotic as she sat on Ethan's lap, clutching him as if she were a child, listening to him whisper meaningless phrases.

She didn't feel like a child, though. Ethan's fingers were firm. His right hand gripped her steadily, keeping her anchored, secure. His left palm stroked her back with a soothing pressure.

No. Not soothing. There was more than that.

His flesh spoke to hers. He had dragged her back from the brink of a nightmare, his steady hands returning her to her body. He had brought her to wakefulness, and then to something more.

Another stroke. Her spine quivered, eager to meet his touch. Heat leached through her body and she sighed, releasing the last tendrils of her dream. She melted beneath his ministrations, soaking into him. She shifted, trying to put her arms around his neck.

He froze. His fingers gripped her tight, tattooing the flesh above her hips. She heard him catch his breath, felt every muscle of his body harden into iron.

Ethan grimaced in the dark. One minute, he'd been offering chaste comfort, trying to ease a frightened soul. The next, that frightened soul had sprung to full, sensual life beneath his fingertips, arching to meet his hand, reflexively seeking the pleasure they'd shared in the past.

The last thing Sloane needed now, though, was to realize just how much pleasure he longed to give her. The last thing she needed was to discover how completely she'd aroused him, how hard he was, just beneath her warm, supple flesh, with only a few layers of fabric between them. "Sloane," he breathed, as she pulled back enough to look into his eyes.

"Please," she said, her voice still faintly blurred from sleep. "Kiss me."

The trust in her moonlit gaze nearly made him lose control. It would be so easy to shift her. So easy to fall back on the mattress beside her. So easy to rip away that cotton thing she was wearing, to see her body, ready and ripe, waiting for him, *eager* for him.

The unbearably rough fabric of his silk boxers taunted him. The feel of her across his lap was almost enough to spring him, to release him from the delicious tension that threatened all his logic, all his higher senses.

Sure, he had told her that she was the one in control.

He had said that she must ask him before he'd give in to his temptation. And he'd heard her words, just a heartbeat before, heard her beg him to touch his lips to hers.

But this wasn't right. This wasn't how he'd envisioned her coming to him. Inviting him, giving up her silly, stubborn rules. She was still dazed, confused by her dream. She wasn't capable of making a true decision.

Summoning the last vestige of his control, he lifted her from his lap. The motion brought him dangerously close to her throat, to the devastatingly smooth stretch of flesh that begged to be tasted, nibbled, nipped. Clenching his teeth, he settled her on the bed. Before she could register the change in their positions, before she could protest, he got to his feet, sucking in his breath against his body's own complaint. He was actually in pain as he made himself move to the far side of the bed, as he gathered up her sheets, as he aired out the linen between them, using it as a shield.

By the time the fabric had drifted on top of her, by the time it had billowed and collapsed and revealed her lithe form, he had enough control over himself that he could speak without groaning. "There's a night-light in the bathroom. I'll turn it on." He matched action to narration, relieved to find that he could walk without betraying his arousal. With half the room between them, he dared to look back at her. She was propped up on her pillows, enthroned like some sort of devastating princess. He could just make out the blue of her eyes in the glow of the night-light from the marble room.

"I'll have James call someone about the tree tomorrow."

"Thank you," she said, and he could hear the confusion in her voice, the question that she was afraid to ask, the invitation that she wanted to issue again. The invitation that he could not accept honorably. Not that night. Not under those circumstances.

"Good night, Sloane," he said as he crossed to her bedroom door.

"Good night," she whispered.

He closed the door behind him as softly as he could. A part of him longed to stand there, to listen until he heard her even breaths, to peek in once she was safely dreaming.

Another part of him, though, knew that he would never be able to walk out of that room again. Not without claiming everything she had to offer. Not without taking away the promise he had given her the night that she had agreed to become his wife.

He curled his hands into fists and made his way down the hall to his own lonely room.

Chapter Four

Sloane poured herself a cup of peppermint tea from the pot that James had set on the countertop. The man had greeted her cheerfully when she padded into the kitchen, her clothes cautiously chosen, hair carefully brushed. A cardamom coffee cake rested on the center island, fragrant as it cooled to eating temperature.

"I hope that you slept well," James said, gesturing for her to pull up one of the nearby bar stools.

Sloane settled onto the comfortable chair and forced herself to take a soothing sip of tea. She wished she could have a healthy dose of caffeine, something to help her wake up after her long night of tossing and turning. She made some noncommittal noise, though. There was no reason to tell James about her strange dreams. No reason to mention Ethan's late-night visit. Before she could weave a polite lie, though, Ethan's unexpected voice sliced across the kitchen. "I want that oak tree down by nightfall, James."

Sloane's gaze shot up from her stoneware mug. Her stomach flipped at the sight of Ethan, framed in the doorway to the kitchen. She'd seen him in a tuxedo, of course. Twice. And in a business suit. But this was the first time she'd seen him in casual clothes. His jeans were snug around his waist, just tight enough to suggest the muscles she knew stretched beneath them. His arms were akimbo, as if he expected to be challenged about the tree. She swallowed hard, trying not to think about the hard abs beneath his hunter-green shirt, the pecs that she had felt under her cheek the night before.

"Of course," James said, his voice calm and respectful. "I'll make the call now."

"It's Sunday," Sloane said. She couldn't imagine what an emergency tree crew would charge on a weekend. "Surely it can wait until tomorrow."

"No," Ethan contradicted. "It can't." He nodded to James, and the caretaker hurried away to solve the problem. Sloane drowned her discomfort in another sip of peppermint tea.

Ethan took advantage of the uneasy silence to pick up the palm-size box on the corner of the center island, the one he had deposited there when he'd returned home from the office the night before. "Here," he said, passing it across to Sloane. She looked up in surprise, peering at him over the rim of her mug. The pose made her look impish. Attractive, in a coltish way.

Damn! What *didn't* make her look attractive? For the hundredth time, he wondered where he'd found the willpower to walk away from her the night before, to honor his promise to stay chaste.

"What's this?" she asked.

"A cell phone. One where the paparazzi can't track you down. My private number is already programmed in."

She picked up the phone with an air of caution. "It's Sunday morning. I just called you yesterday, and you worked until midnight. When did you have time to pick up a new phone?"

He snorted. "That one came under the category of 'security.' Daniel took care of it when he got back to the office, after bringing you here." He reached into his back pocket, taking out his sleek leather wallet. An extra credit card was nestled beside his own. "Now *this* took a little more doing."

He passed the silver card to her. Recognition dawned as she read her name in the raised letters across the bottom. "You can't—" she started to protest.

"I have." He shook his head firmly. "It's a lot easier than my leaving hundred-dollar bills lying around, isn't it?"

There. She was blushing again. He *knew* that he'd made a mistake when he'd left her the money. Then again, if his misstep could bring that defiant sparkle to her eyes...

"Ethan," she said, trying to give him back the card. "Really. This is too much."

He closed his fingers over hers, trying to ignore the hum that her skin ignited in his. "Don't say that. You're going to need it. You have a lot of work ahead of you."

"Work?"

"Daniel took care of the press yesterday. And they definitely know better than to try to get in here." He paused, giving her a moment to think about what he was going to say. He felt guilty for having created the public spectacle that had already changed her life. His past was catching up with him—all those nights of flirting with the press, of tweaking his grandmother's sensibilities, just because he could. If he hadn't invested so much energy and effort into squiring meaningless women around town…

But he hadn't known that he'd meet anyone worth leaving the games behind. He hadn't known Sloane Davenport.

"You're going to need a whole new wardrobe," he said. "Invitations will come in once we announce the engagement, once we make it more official than this morning's gossip columns. Cocktail parties, dinner parties… Your dance card will be full. Buy what you want. Just make sure that one outfit is…sedate."

"Sedate?" She almost laughed, almost thought that he was teasing. But she could hear the tension in his voice. "Why sedate?"

He swallowed hard. "You'll wear it to meet my grandmother. She can be…a challenge."

Sloane almost laughed at the uneasy expression on Ethan's face. She wasn't afraid of Margaret Hartwell. She'd learned all about the woman, before the AFAA charity auction. As project coordinator, Sloane had discovered Margaret's favorite drink was gin and tonic, with extra ice and three limes. She knew that Margaret preferred ballpoint pens to roller balls, that she chose black ink over blue. Margaret's favorite color was green, and her birthday was January 5.

"I'm sure I'll find something she'll approve of," Sloane said. Even if she had to look in the maternity section of the store.

Ethan nodded, as if he were checking off another item on his efficient to-do list. She watched as he crossed the kitchen, then opened a drawer to select a knife. He carved up James's coffee cake with flawless efficiency, placing a generous slice on a plate and passing it to her.

"Oh, that's too much," she said. "I don't usually eat breakfast."

"Well, that will change now."

She bristled at his peremptory tone. "I can decide what I want to eat and what I don't want to eat."

"You could, when you were making decisions for yourself. You've got the baby to think about now."

She made a face. "And the *baby* wants me to eat cardamom coffee cake?"

"Good point. I'll tell James to forget about baking for the next six months. Protein will be good for all of us."

She thought about arguing—she *liked* cardamom coffee cake—but she knew that Ethan was right. In fact, she was secretly pleased that he was concerned about her and the baby's health. And she loved the way that he said "all of us." Loved it so much that she almost missed his question. "Did you get any sleep at all?"

The question was innocent enough—almost the same as James had asked—but it made her remember the feeling of Ethan's arms around her, the heat of his hands burning through her cotton nightgown. She couldn't control the blush that painted her cheeks as she fumbled for an answer. "Yes," she managed. "After a while." After he'd left. After the blood pounding in her veins had finally calmed to a dull roar. She forced herself to meet his gaze. "Thank you," she said.

Thank you for waking me from my nightmare, she meant. Thank you for holding me when I felt like a lost child. Thank you for leaving, when I forgot my promise to myself, when I forgot that I can't have you. Not until we're actually married. Until I'm certain that this is real.

She wanted to say all that. All that and more. But the words jumbled together inside her head, tumbling over one another, until she wasn't sure that she could ever make him understand.

"You're welcome," he said gravely.

She sighed in contentment. He *did* understand. Just as he had when they'd spent hour after hour sharing their thoughts, their secrets, their dreams.

He kept his eyes on hers as he said, "New beds can take some getting used to."

There. That was another conversational gift. He was giving her an option. She could take the easy way out and say something simple and sly and sexy about new beds. They'd laugh together. She'd probably blush.

But he was inviting her to tell him something more. He was opening the door to a deeper conversation, to an admission about the roots of her nightmare. She swallowed hard, then raised her chin, meeting his eyes with a new-forged determination that felt almost like defiance. "You'd think I would have learned to adjust when I was a kid. I was in and out of a lot of foster homes."

She saw the way he was listening to her. She was certain that he'd been about to pour himself a cup of coffee. Instead, he took a casual seat on one of the high stools, hooking his toes under the footrest. His voice was mild as he said, "That must have been difficult."

Trust, Sloane had written. She wanted to trust the man who was going to be her husband. Respect. Partnership.

She needed to make those words happen before she could even tell him that she'd put them on the list, that she'd created a list in the first place. Trust. She raised her chin and said, "There was a woman I used to call Angry Mother."

Ethan merely met her gaze. Sloane hurried on, before she could think about the fact that she had never told anyone about Angry Mother. "That was my third foster home. The house was a wreck, and the windows were all crooked inside their frames. It was freezing at night, all of January, of February. And every morning, Angry Mother told me I was bad, because I tried to sleep in my blue jeans. She put me back in the system because of that. She said I wasn't good enough to keep."

"I'm sorry," Ethan whispered. "No child should have to experience that sort of thing."

It hurt him to see the way that she swallowed, the way that she fought to meet his gaze. Then and there, he promised himself that he would never do anything to make her look that bleak again. Gently, he said, "Your parents..." He trailed off, giving her the option of picking up the words, of sharing more of her story, her past.

"I never knew my father. I think he was a lot older than my mother. He was long gone by the time I was born." He watched Sloane's fingers curl over her belly, as if she were protecting their baby from an ugly truth. Her voice was a lot harder when she said, "My mother was only seventeen when she had me. She was an addict and she'd already been in and out of treatment for three years when I came along. She stayed clean, though, the entire time she was carrying me."

"She must have loved you very much." He said the words because he knew they had to be true. It twisted his heart when Sloane shook her head.

"She put me into foster care before I was a year old."

She tried to be matter-of-fact, but he heard the carefully trained acceptance in her tone. Old doubt was transparent in her eyes; it weighted down her shoulders. He tried to keep his own tone light as he contradicted. "But she put you first, for nine months. Keeping away from drugs for her pregnancy couldn't have been easy, especially when she was only a child herself. She wanted you to be healthy. Safe."

Sloane had never thought about it that way. All these years, she'd thought about her mother as a weak person, a sick woman, unable to face the new life that she'd created through her own mistakes. Sloane had never once seen her mother as strong or brave. Doing what she thought best, even when everyone had turned against her, had left her on her own.

As Sloane met Ethan's steady gaze, another piece of the puzzle dropped into place. "She wanted to get me back. She put me in foster care because she thought that she'd get better, that she'd get well enough for us to live together. She could have put me up for adoption, but she hoped…"

Hope. The word was a strange one when applied to Sloane's childhood. *Hope* wasn't a word that Sloane associated with the dark-haired woman she barely remembered. *Hope* wasn't part of her foster family patchwork.

But it was, of course. It had been all along. That was why Sloane had named her internet work the Hope Project. That was why she had designed her system, to help children like she had been.

"Thank you," she said to Ethan. "I hadn't really thought about things that way before."

She was warmed by his easy smile. "Glad that I could be of assistance." He lifted the teapot that James had left on the counter, gesturing toward her mug. "Can I heat that up for you?"

She edged the stoneware closer to him. "You're spoiling me."

"That's my intention."

She flushed at the purr beneath his words. She would have gulped down her tea, but she knew that it would burn her tongue. She settled for using her fork to tamp down stray crumbs from her coffee cake. When the silence ticked a dozen points closer to unbearable, she blurted out, "What about you? You said that your grandmother raised you?"

Damn. Ethan would rather spend the morning teasing her, bringing out that blush on her cheeks. He'd even prefer talking about *her* past, navigating the thicket of her tangled family ties. Turnabout was fair play, though. "My parents got divorced when I was seven. Neither of them was prepared to raise a…challenging child alone, so Grandmother stepped in."

"Challenging?"

"Let's just say that I didn't like to follow the rules very much."

"Didn't?" She raised her eyebrows and extended her hand toward him, so that her engagement ring sparkled in the morning sunlight. "I don't think that's changed very much, Mr. Hartwell. You and rules still seem to be pretty much strangers to each other."

"Why change when something's working for you?" he retorted with a shrug. She should smile more often. It brought out the sparkle in her eyes.

"Seriously," she said, taking back her hand before he could think of something distracting to do with those long fingers. "What sort of trouble did you get into?"

"Let's just say that my grandmother ended up on a first-name basis with the principal." Sloane's lips quirked in amusement. "At all five schools I attended." She grinned. "And the Coast Guard commander who tracked down my sailboat when I tried to run away from home." She laughed. "For the third time."

He'd gone too far there. Told too much. Sloane wasn't a fool; she obviously heard the darker story beneath his joking. She immediately seemed to grasp that no boy caused *that* much trouble unless there was something very wrong in his life. A frown ironed a crease between her eyebrows. "Why so desperate to get away?"

He still could laugh it off. It wasn't too late to make up something ridiculous about being a bad boy, about playing a rogue-in-training. He had planned to keep things light, to make everything easy, for another three weeks at least, until the prenatal testing could be done.

But Sloane would remember this conversation when he finally told her the truth. She would recall all the things he'd told her, and the huge, important things he'd left unsaid. She would conclude that he had lied to her, by omission, at the very least. He took a deep breath, wishing that it was late enough in the day to break out a bottle of Scotch, to fortify himself for this conversation that he absolutely did not want to have, that he'd never wanted to share with anyone.

Sloane felt Ethan's mood shift, as if a cloud had scudded across the sun. Even though he didn't move, she felt him withdraw from her. For just a heartbeat, she thought that he was going to slip beneath the mask of Bachelor of the Year, to shift back to the good-times-guy she had read about in the paper, the one who belonged at AFAA charity auctions every night of the year.

Instead, he reached for her hand, folding his fingers around hers with an urgency that sent her heart leaping into her throat. "Sloane," he said. "We have to talk."

She forced her lips to turn up at the corners even though the fake grin made her throat ache. "No good conversation ever started that way."

She tried to pull her hand away, but he wouldn't let

her go. Instead, he took a deep breath, then exhaled on a count of five. "I wasn't an only child, Sloane. I had a brother and a sister, but they both died, before I was five. That was what pulled my parents apart. That was why I spent so much time acting out."

She heard the sorrow behind his words, still raw after all those years. She blinked, taking in the grand kitchen, the fine mansion that surrounded her. Of course, money truly couldn't buy happiness. It hadn't been able to spare the Hartwells from tragedy. "What happened?" she asked, her mind skirting over a dozen terrible accidents.

"My brother and sister were born with a genetic mutation, trisomy. She lived for almost three years, but he survived only a few days."

Genetic mutation.

The words were ugly, frightening—all the more so for the irony that Ethan's company was Hartwell Genetics, a forerunner in creating cures for terrible diseases. No, Sloane realized. It wasn't ironic at all. Those poor siblings were the reason that Hartwell Genetics flourished. Ethan had devoted his life to saving other families the agony that his own had suffered. Ethan, and his grandmother, too. How long had the company been in existence? How long had they fought to find a cure?

Sloane suddenly realized what Ethan was going to say next. Her fingers clutched at her blouse, closing over the delicate life that grew inside her.

No. She had to be wrong. *Ethan* was fine. He didn't have...what was it? Trisomy? It couldn't kill every child in the family. It couldn't put an end to the entire Hartwell line. It absolutely, positively couldn't affect the baby she had already come to love so much.

She forced herself to ask, "It runs in your family, then?"

He nodded, his hazel eyes nearly black. When he spoke, he sounded as if he were making a solemn vow. "Sloane, I never meant for this to happen. I never intended to have children at all. You know I took precautions—" His throat closed around that last word, and all she could do was clutch his fingers where they still grasped hers. He steadied himself with another deep breath, and then he squared his shoulders. "There are tests now. They can do amnio at fourteen weeks."

"Fourteen," she said, trying to absorb everything he had told her. That left three weeks hanging in the balance. Three weeks of not knowing.

He nodded, raising his free hand to her cheek. "That was why I told you I wanted the paternity test. That is what I really need to know."

Sloane felt light-headed. She had been so worried that Ethan didn't trust her. She had tried to convince herself that his insistence on a paternity test was to protect himself, to protect the Hartwell family fortune. Now, her heart leaped at the notion that *trust* wasn't the issue at all. Ethan *did* believe her.

But any relief was crushed by darker thoughts. Their child could be in the worst kind of danger. She pulled away from his caress, extracting her hand from his grasp. "Why didn't you tell me before?"

"I didn't want to worry you. I didn't want you to be afraid."

"Ethan, I think this is something worth worrying about! This disease has destroyed your family! I had a right to know!"

"How was that supposed to work?" he snapped. "What was I supposed to say? 'Marry me? And by the way, our babies might all die'?"

She heard the self-hatred behind his words, recognized the emotion for what it was. Nevertheless, she said, "You could have held off on the 'marry me' part! At the very least, you could have told me the truth!"

"You don't understand! I watched this thing ruin my parents' marriage! I watched it tear them apart! I wanted to prove that I could do this. That I could be better than they were."

"All the more reason that you should have told me, Ethan." He started to interrupt, but she pressed on. "You're right, you know. Our story can be different from theirs. I'm not your mother. You're not your father. Our baby isn't your sister or your brother."

She saw that his immediate reaction was to fight. As she watched, though, he swallowed one retort, then another. He spread his fingers across the granite countertop, as if he were seeking strength from the cool stone. He nodded slowly, and then he said, "You're right. I should have told you. And in the interest of full disclosure now, you should know that I've made an appointment with Dr. Morton for three weeks from tomorrow. I'll need a copy of your obstetrician's reports from your other visits. I want to get those to Phil tomorrow morning."

"Phil?" She could think of about a dozen things wrong with Ethan's request, but the first word to splutter from her lips was the unfamiliar name.

"Phillip Morton. He's the leading obstetrician in D.C. He knows my family history. He'll take over your case now."

She wanted to say that she was perfectly content with her own doctor. She wanted to say that she had everything under control.

But she didn't.

She'd only been to the doctor once since finding out

she was pregnant. That was all she'd been able to afford. She swallowed hard and met Ethan's eyes, fully aware of the fact that she was about to make her own uncomfortable disclosure. "Fine. I'll switch to Dr. Morton. But there aren't a lot of records. I've only been to the obstetrician once."

He couldn't have been more surprised if she'd slapped him. "What?" he asked, half expecting to find that he'd misheard. A woman as fiercely devoted to her unborn baby as Sloane... Only going to the doctor once in her entire first trimester? "Standard medical protocol—" he started to recite.

She cut him off. "Standard medical protocol has insurance. At the very least, it has a job. I've been doing everything that I'm supposed to do," she said. "I've read all the books, and there are all sorts of communities online. I was very active in one of them before..."

He barely smothered his sigh of frustration when she trailed off. "Before what?"

"Before my computer died." She looked away, as if she were confessing infidelity. "I've been going down to the public library, though. Everything I've experienced with this pregnancy has been textbook perfect. They could write a book about me."

He heard a suspicious brightness behind her tone, and he wondered if she was trying to convince him, or just herself.

He had a choice. He could push her about the doctor visits, about the limited care that she'd provided for their child. He could lambaste her for managing her life so poorly that she had nothing in reserve, no savings to fall back on. He could vent some of the fierce possessiveness that clenched his fists, the driving need to keep her safe, to protect her, to ease her way. He could take out on her all of his fear about the Hartwell genetic curse, all of his anxiety about the unknown state of their baby.

Or he could let it go.

There wasn't any way to change the past. No way to pick up the missing appointments. Besides, who was he to say that *she* had been irresponsible? She'd managed to keep a roof over her head for nearly three months, without a job. She'd done the best she could under challenging circumstances. He exhaled slowly and forced himself to release the tension that torqued his shoulders. "Okay," he said. And then, because she was sitting there, obviously nervous and clearly still processing the bombshell he had dropped in the middle of their Sunday brunch, he asked, "Did you bring your computer from your apartment?"

She nodded. "It's upstairs."

"I'll take it into the office tomorrow. Someone in the computer department should be able to fix it. At the very least, they can transfer everything from your hard drive to a new machine."

He made the offer so casually. Just as he'd presented her with the cell phone, with the credit card. Sloane had spent weeks worrying about her failing computer; she'd wasted hours wondering what she was going to do when the thing finally refused to turn on at all. She was so close to launching the Hope Project....

And just like that, he could give her back all the tools she needed. He could make things right.

If only their visit to Dr. Morton resolved problems as easily... "Ethan," she said, but then she realized that she didn't know what she wanted to ask. She smoothed her blouse over her belly, wishing that the pregnancy was already further along, wishing that she could feel the reassuring flutter of a new life inside her.

He settled his hand over hers. Strength flowed through his fingers. Strength and an iron-firm resolve. "Ask me any questions, Sloane. I'll tell you the truth, as best I can."

She wanted numbers. She wanted absolutes. She wanted guarantees. But she knew that he could never give her those. "We'll know the test results in three weeks?"

He shook his head. "Phil will do the amnio then. It takes time for the cells to be cultured, for results to come in. Probably another ten days."

She had to ask the next question, even though she dreaded the answer. "And if we get bad news?"

A nerve twitched beneath his right eye. She saw him withdraw, disappear into his memories, into the past of a family torn apart by *bad news*. When he answered, his voice was barely a whisper. "I can't do it, Sloane. I'm not strong enough to be a father for that kind of child. A child that we know we're going to lose, probably much sooner rather than later."

She knew she should be grateful that he was answering her honestly. She should welcome the unvarnished truth, even though it hurt him to say the words, even though her heart pounded in her chest when she realized what he meant. She had to answer him, though. She had to tell him how *she* felt. "Ethan, I am never giving up this baby."

"Sloane, you don't understand. You can't imagine what it's like—"

She wasn't angry with him. She wasn't afraid. She wasn't even overwhelmed by sorrow. She just knew that she was determined, that she was absolutely, one hundred percent certain. "No, Ethan. That isn't a possibility."

He ran his hand through his hair, making the golden strands stand on end. "Let's wait and see. Let's wait until we have all the facts."

She didn't need anymore facts.

Before she could drive home the point, though, the doorbell rang. Sloane heard James greet someone in the foyer. There was easy laughter, comfortable familiarity. She glanced at Ethan, saw his face brighten. He shot Sloane a quick glance, and she shrugged. They could finish their conversation another time. Not that there was anything left to say. Not before they had test results in hand.

"Zach!" Ethan exclaimed, as a man walked into the kitchen. The newcomer was Ethan's opposite in every way. His hair was dark where Ethan's was light; his eyes were ordinary brown instead of Ethan's complicated hazel. Zach was short, and he could easily stand to lose twenty pounds. His T-shirt was wrinkled, as if he'd pulled it out of a laundry hamper, and his jeans slouched around his hips.

"Zachary Crosby, this is Sloane Davenport. Sloane, Zach." Zach's hand was soft in hers, but he smiled as he said hello. As Zach reached for a coffee cup, Ethan said wryly, "Make yourself at home." The newcomer was clearly familiar with the Hartwell kitchen; he wasted no time collecting a plate and a fork, cutting himself a generous slice of the cardamom coffee cake.

He downed a huge bite, chasing it with a hefty swallow of coffee. He might act like a starved teenager, but Sloane quickly realized that there was more to the man than met the casual eye. His glance darted to the cell phone that still sat on the center island, to the silver credit card beside it. He scarcely missed a beat before zeroing in on her left hand, on the diamond ring that glinted in the morning light.

"Then the rumors are true. I take it congratulations are in order," he said, shifting his gaze from Sloane to Ethan.

Ethan stared at him for a long moment. Some silent communication passed between the men, an entire conversation, made easy by their obvious familiarity. Ethan finally said, "Sloane and I got engaged on Friday night."

"Have you set a date yet?"

Sloane thought the question was a little odd, especially since it was directed at Ethan. Dates were something women asked about, girlfriends, excited about a wedding in the offing. She thought about her list. June 1—the earliest date that made any sense at all.

Before she could decide whether or not to say anything, Ethan replied, "Nothing certain." His tone was terse.

Another glance passed between the two men, another flash of communication. Sloane wasn't certain what Ethan was saying, what the meaning was behind his words. That was silly, though. There wasn't any secret meaning. They *hadn't* decided on a date.

Zach just nodded, as if he'd expected the answer. "Don't worry," he said. "I'll have my best man's toast ready, whatever date you choose." His sudden smile brightened the entire room. "Just think of the stories I can finally make public...."

Ethan rolled his eyes as he said to Sloane, "Don't believe a word this guy tells you. He's the worst liar I've ever known."

Zach only laughed. "Twenty-five years of being your best friend, and this is the way I'm treated?" He passed his mug to Ethan, waiting for a refill. "Besides, you should be especially nice to me today. I brought you a present."

"I can't wait," Ethan said dryly.

Zach glanced toward the foyer. "James! You can bring her in!"

Her?

Afterward, Sloane couldn't have said what she had thought she would see. There was always the specter of Ethan's old girlfriends. Or his grandmother. Or even some business associate, waiting to steal him away for whatever was left of the weekend.

But Sloane had never expected a *puppy*. A fuzzy, black-and-white bundle of fur, with paws the size of dinner plates.

"What the—" Ethan exclaimed, even as Sloane knelt beside the excited dog.

"May I present Heritage Sacre Bleu Chevalier? Or, you can just call her Daisy."

"What type of dog is she?" Sloane asked, as the puppy licked her fingers with unbridled enthusiasm.

"A purebred Old English sheepdog. Eight weeks old." Zach laughed as Ethan swore under his breath. "You won the silent auction bid, and now she's all yours. I've got her official papers out in the car, along with a leash and some Puppy Chow. Congratulations."

"You can take your official papers, and—"

"The Ballet Fund is truly grateful for your very generous gift, Mr. Hartwell."

Zach sounded as pious as an altar boy. James chuckled from the doorway. Sloane caught her breath, waiting to see what Ethan would do, how he would react to the surprise.

For a moment, his face was dark, frustration twisting his features. But then, he looked at Sloane. She felt him measure her smile. She saw him register her fingers already twined in the puppy's soft fur. She watched him turn to Zach, shaking his head. "You're going to owe me for this one, buddy. Owe me, big time."

Daisy chose that moment to deliver one short bark, as if she understood every word of the mock threat. Sloane watched in amusement as Ethan Hartwell, M.D., MBA, president of Hartwell Genetics knelt down beside her, accepting a slobbery canine kiss from the newest member of his family.

Chapter Five

Three nights later, Sloane plucked at her blouse, removing a glistening white strand of Daisy's fur from the aquamarine silk. Ethan grinned openly at the gesture; he had already fought his own good-natured battle against the puppy's long fur before they'd left the house. "I thought that Old English sheepdogs don't shed," Sloane said.

"They don't lose their winter coats all at once in the spring, like some dogs. Instead, they drop hair all year round."

Sloane raised her eyebrows. "It sounds like you've been doing some research."

"What else would a responsible dog owner do?" Ethan shrugged as he helped himself to a generous bite of his duck à l'orange.

Sloane smiled at his offhand acceptance of the responsibility that Zach had thrust upon them. Ethan might have grumbled about the puppy initially, but he'd certainly been in a great mood for the past three days.

His impromptu invitation to a Wednesday night dinner had come as a complete surprise. At first, Sloane had protested when he named the restaurant—the French country inn was known to be one of the most expensive places in the Washington area. Ethan had insisted, though, saying that he wanted her to try the white asparagus in one of the inn's famous appetizers.

He'd been right, of course. The food was incredible. Her scallops were divine, in their complicated sauce of shrimp, oranges and olives. "How is your duck?" she asked.

Before Ethan could answer, though, Sloane's cell phone rang. She wrinkled her nose in embarrassment, realizing she should have put the thing on vibrate before they even set foot inside the exclusive restaurant. The ringtone grew louder as she rifled through her handbag, taking some things out to speed her getting to the phone. A hand mirror jostled the spoon beside her plate, quickly followed by lipstick, a pen and a carefully folded piece of paper.

At last, she got to the phone, only to see the cheerful icon that told her she had missed a call. She glanced at the phone number and realized it started with 1-800— no one she actually knew at all.

"Sorry," she said ruefully, thumbing the switch to set the phone to vibrate.

"No problem." Ethan's smile was easy. She started to squirrel away her possessions, but he reached out to grab the sheet of paper. "What's this?"

Her stomach plummeted. "It's nothing," she said, trying to keep her voice light.

"It has my name on it."

Of course it had his name on it. She'd typed his name when she'd made up the list, the catalog of what she wanted out of their relationship. She had kept the page in her purse, afraid to leave it anywhere that James or Ethan or anyone else could stumble upon it.

Just as Ethan had done now.

"Please," she said. "It's nothing. It's just a stupid note I wrote to myself."

His voice was gently teasing. "Should I be offended that my name is on a 'stupid' note?"

She felt color flood her cheeks. *Respect.* That was on the list, wasn't it? She needed Ethan to respect her. Even when she did silly things like write up a list of traits she needed for their marriage to work. Well, this would be a great test.

She swallowed hard, and then she nodded toward the paper. "Go ahead, then. Read it." She gulped at her sparkling water as he took his time absorbing the five words. Five words and a date.

His hazel eyes were serious as they met hers. "What does it mean?"

"It's what I want, Ethan. What I need. If we're ever going to make this work, really work, long term."

"Trust?" he asked, and his voice was surprisingly, impossibly gentle.

If he'd taken any other tone, she would have challenged him. As it was, his tenderness made her feel shy. She stared down at her plate, as if she could make out some magic reply amid the seafood. "You frighten me," she finally said.

Out of the corner of her eye, she saw him draw back, pull away as if she'd burned him. She glanced up just in time to catch the look of shock on his face, of something stronger—something she might even call horror.

"No!" she hastened to clarify. "Not frighten me, like I'm afraid you'll hurt me." But then she had to explain some more. "Not hurt me physically. I know you would never do that. But Ethan, I know your reputation—the women, the parties, the constant social life. I knew it when I met you and I'm so afraid that nothing has changed. That nothing will ever change."

His eyes softened as she fumbled for the words. "Sloane," he said, reaching across the table to twine his fingers between hers. "There isn't anyone else. There hasn't been since you agreed to wear my ring. There won't be. Not ever. I promise."

When she still hesitated, he reached into the breast pocket of his jacket, fished out his personal cell phone, the one that he used for private calls, separate and apart from Hartwell Genetics business. Still holding her gaze, he dropped it into the ice bucket beside their table, using her bright green bottle of sparkling water to push the electronic device to the bottom of its icy grave.

"Ethan!"

"If I kept an actual little black book, I would give it to you to burn."

"Ethan, you didn't have to do that!" But she was laughing.

"That brings us to…" He looked back at her creased page. "Respect."

Amusement died on her lips. "I'm never going to be famous like all those other women you've known. I need to know that you can respect what I am—a simple woman who wants to help people, help children. A woman who is never going to be an actress, or a model or anybody special."

Anybody special. Did Sloane have any idea what she was saying? Ethan saw the earnestness in her face, felt her urgency like a palpable thing as she waited for him to respond.

His first instinct was to laugh. Of *course* he respected her. How could he not respect a woman who knew what she wanted in life and took the difficult steps to get there? She had paid her own way through college, through graduate school, all so that she had the credentials she needed to make her dream come true. She had taken a meaningless gofer job and turned it into a dynamic position at the foundation, a coordinator's post that had netted hundreds of thousands of dollars for the organization in a single night.

But laughter would destroy Sloane now. Laughter was the last thing that she needed from him. The last thing that he would ever give her. He leaned over the table, lowering his voice so that she needed to move closer as well, so that she met him partway.

"Sloane Davenport, I respect you. I respect you, and everything that you are trying to do. I respect your work on the Hope Project."

He couldn't leave it at that, though. Because he did respect her mind, he did respect her drive, but she pulled an equally strong response from him in other ways. He roughened his tone until his words were almost a growl. "And I respect the fact that you got me to make a promise up there, on the Kennedy Center terrace. You got me to vow not to take you into my bed until after we marry. Any woman who can drive a bargain that…" He cleared his throat, making his meaning absolutely, perfectly, one hundred percent clear. "That…persuasively, gains my absolute, undying respect."

She blinked hard at the innuendo behind his words. His tone, though, freed something inside her. Like a zipper easing down, metal foot by metal foot, she felt tension flow from her shoulders. She had not realized how much she wanted to talk to him about her list, how much she had needed to share her needs. Her desires.

That sense of release gave her the courage to say, "That leaves us with the last thing. Partnership. I need to know we're equals in this."

"Does that mean you're offering to walk Daisy when she gets up in the middle of the night?"

Her smile was fleeting. "I mean it, Ethan. We need to work together, to know each other well enough that we can stand side by side, through anything."

He leaned back in his chair, shrugging and spreading his hands to either side. "Fine. Ask me anything. What do you want to know?"

There were a thousand things, of course. She started with the first thing that came to mind. "What was your favorite toy when you were growing up?"

"My chemistry set. After Grandmother got over the first three explosions."

"What's your favorite book?"

"John Steinbeck's *East of Eden*."

"Your favorite color?"

"Blue."

"Why didn't you have a vasectomy, years ago? Why did you ever take a chance at getting some woman pregnant, if you were so worried about passing along the genes?"

The question surprised her as much as it surprised him. She had been thinking it for days, though, ever since he had told her about the danger. Ever since he had sparked the constant gnawing uncertainty about the health of their baby, the niggling fear that would not be put to rest for several more weeks.

"I'm sorry," she said, when she saw the stricken look on his face. "You don't have to answer that."

"No." He drew a deep breath, and then he took a healthy swallow of his burgundy. "I do." He rubbed his hand across his mouth, as if the gesture would help him to collect his thoughts. "I never had the surgery because it would be permanent. It felt like giving up. Like admitting that we'll never find a cure."

"After what? Fifty years?"

He heard what she was doing with her voice, the way she tried to be gentle with him. The way she tried to say that there might not ever be a cure. He appreciated the effort, even as he pushed away her specific question.

"In fifty years, Hartwell Genetics has brought hundreds of new pharmaceuticals to the market. We've found cures for a dozen different diseases. We've helped millions of people. We just haven't helped my family. Yet."

"Yet," she said, purposely hardening her voice to match his certainty.

He nodded, and then he rubbed his hands together, obviously closing the door on that part of their conversation. *For now,* he amended mentally. Until Sloane decided that she needed to talk about it again. He would answer any questions that she had, whenever she had them. He would do that for her.

"Your turn," he said with a devilish smile. "What's your favorite dessert?"

"Chocolate mousse," she said. "No, wait! Crème caramel!"

"Let's see what we can do about that then, shall we?" He raised his chin, claiming the attention of the waiter on the far side of the room.

Hours later, well after crème caramel and coffee

and several long, lingering kisses, Sloane was falling asleep in the privacy of the guest suite when she remembered the last thing on her list—the June wedding date. Oh, well, she thought, already slipping into the fuzzy warmth of a dream. There was plenty of time to set a date…months and months and months.

Sloane caught her tongue between her teeth, holding her breath as she pressed the enter key on her computer. A progress bar appeared on the screen, racing from left to right, and then a model of the Hope Project home page blinked into existence. Every photograph was in place. The fonts were correct. Three columns marched neatly across the screen.

"Yes!" she cried, pumping her fist in the air. She was startled to hear laughter from the doorway. "Ethan!" she exclaimed, looking up. "How long have you been standing there?"

He ignored her question. "I take it the Hope Project is going well?"

He looked perfectly relaxed in his broadcloth shirt and tailored trousers, as if he'd left the office hours before. She wondered what he was doing home in the middle of the day, on a Friday no less. Glancing back at her computer screen, she grinned. "I finally got the front page to look the way I want it to. It's taken about a hundred tries, but everything is finally falling into place." Ethan started to walk across the library, but she shielded the screen with her palms. "No! You can't look at it yet. It's not ready for prime time."

He held up his hands as if to prove that he was innocent. "The computer's working all right, then?"

"It's wonderful." She couldn't help but caress the sleek silver edge of the casing. The new machine was ten times faster than the wreck she'd brought from her apartment. Ethan had assured her that the computer was just something he'd had lying around the office, that it hadn't cost him a penny. Reluctantly, she'd accepted it, telling herself that she needed *something* to help her fill the long hours that he spent at the office. Speaking of which... "What are you doing home?"

"Don't we have Daisy's appointment this afternoon?"

The puppy's first visit to the veterinarian, a simple checkup to make sure she was in general good health. "I thought I was going to take her," Sloane said. James had already told her that she could take the SUV from the garage. Sloane had looked up directions to the vet's office, telling herself that she would have no trouble navigating the unfamiliar streets. No trouble, that was, if Daisy behaved herself.

Ethan shrugged easily. "It didn't seem fair for me to stick you with the hard stuff. Partnership, right? We're in this together."

If Ethan had harbored any doubts about coming home early, they were banished by Sloane's brilliant smile. He really *should* be back at the office, but there would always be time to schedule another meeting with the in-house trademark lawyers.

He watched Sloane's fingers fly over her keyboard, saving whatever she had just completed on her internet project. He was glad that the new machine was working out well. The technology guru back at the office had laughed when Ethan suggested repairing Sloane's old computer. "It'll cost more and take longer for me to order replacement parts for this ancient thing than for you to just buy something new, something top-of-the-line." The guy had shaken his head as if he were studying some museum exhibit on the history of home computing.

Top-of-the-line it had been, then. Getting the new computer was simple enough. And it made Sloane happy.

Ethan produced a ring of keys from the pocket of his trousers. "Do you want to drive? Or should I?"

Sloane told herself that she was silly to feel so relieved. Of course she *could* have made it to the veterinarian's office on her own. Nevertheless, she laughed as she said, "You drive. Our fearless watchdog is in the kitchen, sleeping on her new bed."

She switched off her computer and led the way out of the library. She was pretty sure Ethan was watching her as she walked in front of him. Normally, the thought would have made her self-conscious, but that afternoon, she felt empowered. She had just taken a major step toward completing the Hope Project. She was managing her life, accomplishing her goals. *And* Ethan had remembered the words that she had typed on that slip of paper. He had been the one to say *partnership*.

She let her hips sway a little more than usual as she walked down the hall. She couldn't help but run her fingers through her hair. She slowed her pace, just a fraction.

She widened her eyes with mock innocence, as she tried to convince herself that it wouldn't be *her* fault if Ethan came up close behind her. *She* wouldn't be responsible if he nuzzled that sensitive place at the side of her throat, if he started to play with the buttons on her floral blouse. If he tempted her to forget every single promise that she'd made to herself and to the baby inside her. At least, it wouldn't be *entirely* her fault. Would it?

Before she could decide just how far she was willing to tempt her fiancé, she was distracted by the sharp yap of an excited puppy, newly energized by a nap.

"Yes," Ethan said, brushing against Sloane before he knelt on the floor to wrestle with the barking hellion. His hand lingered against Sloane's hip for just long enough that she was certain he had been reading her mind. He didn't follow through on that tingling promise, though. Instead, he crooned to Daisy, "I'm home. And you're glad to see me. You know how to welcome a man back to his house."

As Sloane watched, Ethan continued talking to the fluff ball of a dog. He growled at Daisy in mock ferocity as he eased the animal into her harness, double-checking the fastening to make sure the puppy couldn't escape, couldn't come to harm on his watch. The click of Ethan's tongue was automatic as he summoned the dog to walk beside him to the garage. He was a natural at controlling Daisy, at giving her the length of leash she needed, at pulling back to keep her manageable and secure before he put her into a travel crate.

Ethan handled the car with the same smooth efficiency, winding his way through the shady summertime streets. As he braked to a stop at a traffic light, he asked Sloane, "So, how close are you to finishing the Hope Project?"

"Getting that template to work this afternoon was a major step forward. I still need to test the algorithms, though, to make sure that everything works as well online as it does on paper. I'd like to think that it will function perfectly, but there's a huge difference between design and reality."

"Tell me about it." He sighed, heading back into traffic.

"What does that mean?" she asked. "Are you having computer problems at work?"

"Not a computer." He shrugged and glanced in the

rearview mirror before changing lanes. "There's a new drug that showed a lot of promise in the lab. Turns out it's not nearly as effective in our first round of human test subjects. It's safe, not going to hurt anyone. But if it worked as well as it did in the last round of testing, we could wipe out an entire class of diseases."

She heard the disappointment in his voice. There was something else there, though, something that ran even deeper. It took her a moment to process his words, to figure out what she was responding to. Ah, that was it. *Determination.*

Ethan was determined to make his drug therapy work, no matter how many times he had to go back to the drawing board. No matter what it cost him financially, emotionally. He was invested in Hartwell Genetics, and he wouldn't give up until the new drug functioned flawlessly.

Maybe that was what had drawn her to him in the first place. Okay, she reasoned with herself. In the *second* place. She'd been drawn to him in the first place by his incredibly sexy smile, by his ruffled hair, by the smoky way his eyes had tracked her when she'd walked into the Eastern Hotel bar.

His determination was what had convinced her to take the chance of a lifetime, to jump into the deep end by agreeing to marry him when her entire life had turned upside down. Ethan was a man who could make things happen. He could get things done.

Her fingers inched across her blouse, gathering up the fabric in tiny hills and valleys. There were some things, she knew, that even Ethan couldn't accomplish. Their baby was growing, with or without the Hartwell genetic flaw. Ethan couldn't change that. Not now. Not ever. And she dreaded the fight that she knew was coming if all her hopes came to nothing, if all her dreams crumbled to ash with the amnio results that Ethan dreaded. Sloane could barely imagine what life would be like if she were pitted against the very determination that had drawn her in so deeply at the start.

"I lost you there," Ethan said, and she was flustered to realize that he had pulled into a parking space. She had completely lost track of their drive, of the careful twists and turns that had brought them to the vet's office.

"Sorry," she said, flashing him an automatic smile. She wasn't about to tell him all of her worries. No reason to borrow trouble. Not now. As if to emphasize Sloane's resolve, Daisy yipped from her crate in the back of the vehicle. "I didn't mean to zone out like that."

She undid her seat belt with her own gesture of determination. Ethan shot her an appraising look, as if he knew that she was ducking out of an unpleasant conversation. He didn't press the point, though. Instead, he easily maneuvered the latch on Daisy's crate, bundling up the wriggling puppy, laughing as the dog tried to smother him with sloppy kisses.

Soon enough, an only slightly subdued Daisy was standing on the veterinarian's examination table, shaking her head at the scope Dr. Johnson used to inspect her ears. With the vet's right hand firm on her neck, the puppy submitted to having her teeth inspected. "Her gums look good," the vet said. "She should start to lose her milk teeth in a couple of months. She'll chew on things constantly as her adult teeth come in. Make sure she has toys, or you'll find yourself out a pair of shoes or two."

Sloane laughed. "No problem there. She has all the toys a puppy could ever need." Ethan had seen to that, bringing home a wide selection of playthings earlier in the week. Zach might have strong-armed him into accepting the puppy, but Ethan was taking his responsibilities as a pet owner seriously.

Dr. Johnson moved her hands down Daisy's back, apparently pleased with the alignment of the puppy's spine. She reached around to the belly, palpating and nodding to herself. "No masses in the abdomen," the doctor said, before she slipped her stethoscope buds into her ears.

Ethan approved of the doctor's smooth actions. The woman was clearly comfortable with puppies. It was obvious that she liked them; the vet had exclaimed over Daisy as if she were the only dog on the schedule for the entire afternoon.

Comfort, though, and enthusiasm, weren't enough when it came to medical care. A good doctor was thorough. Able to diagnose problems from the subtlest of hints.

Dr. Johnson moved her stethoscope around, finding a better placement on Daisy's chest. A tiny frown tightened around the woman's lips, and she planted the medical instrument again. Another shift, another angle for the stethoscope's round plate.

"Is there something wrong, Doctor?" Ethan made himself keep his voice even, but he felt his brain shift into businessman mode. As an officer of Hartwell Genetics, he was accustomed to dealing with medical professionals who bore bad news. As an expert in human genetics, he was prepared to discuss anatomical anomalies, contraindications, complex diagnoses.

Sloane must have recognized the change in his focus. He heard her breath catch at the back of her throat. Wishing that he could spare her whatever the doctor was about to say, he stepped closer, weaving Sloane's fingers between his own. Her hand was cold, slack, as if she already knew that the veterinarian had bad news.

Dr. Johnson only shook her head, taking several long minutes to listen further to Daisy's chest. When she finally removed the stethoscope from her ears, her face was grave. "I'm sorry," she said. "At first, I wasn't certain what I was hearing—I didn't expect to find it in a puppy this young."

"Find what?" Sloane asked the question before Ethan could, her voice impossibly fragile.

"Daisy has a heart murmur. The valves of her heart aren't functioning the way that they should, so her heart isn't pumping blood as efficiently as normal."

"What grade?" Ethan snapped. He'd read enough laboratory studies over the years to know that there were five grades of heart murmur. Grade one or two, and Daisy was fine; she'd likely grow out of the problem. Three or four, though, and the poor dog would have problems, meaning she'd likely require medication. And five...

"Five," the vet said grimly.

"But what—" Sloane started to ask, her voice breaking before she could complete the question.

"You'll do an EKG to be sure?" Ethan asked. The electrocardiogram might give them valuable information. Let him control the situation. Manage everything that was going wrong.

"Of course," Dr. Johnson said. "And an echocardiogram might get us more information as well. Maybe some X-rays, if it seems like they can give us more facts."

"You have the equipment here?"

"Yes," the veterinarian assured him. "Of course, the tests can become rather expensive—"

"Just do them," Ethan cut her off.

Dr. Johnson flashed him a pleased smile. "Some people aren't willing to invest in a new pet, a puppy they've hardly gotten to know."

"Do whatever tests you need to do," Ethan said.

The vet gathered up the squirming puppy. "Come on, you. These tests aren't going to hurt. And you just might get a treat when we're done." She turned back to Ethan and Sloane. "We'll probably need an hour or two. There's a coffee shop next door, if you want to wait there."

If Ethan had been on his own, he would have insisted on waiting right there in the examining room. Keeping himself front and center, he would have made the vet's staff work harder, complete the tests sooner, interpret the results just a little faster.

One glance at Sloane, though, told Ethan that it would be a mistake to stay there. Her face was rigid with worry. She was already looking at the instruments in the examining room as if they were tools in some medieval torture chamber. It was better for Sloane to get away, to wait somewhere else.

"Thank you," Ethan said stiffly.

The veterinarian smiled, as if she knew the battle he had fought. "Just leave your cell phone number with the receptionist, and we'll call you as soon as we have any results."

This was a nightmare, Sloane thought as she watched the doctor carry off Daisy.

Any minute now, Sloane was going to wake up. She would hear the oak tree scraping against her window, smell the roses on the writing desk. She would realize this was all a bad dream, and she would laugh at herself.

But the oak tree had been cut down almost a week

ago, the very same Sunday that Zach had brought Daisy into their lives. The roses had been replaced with a new floral display, a riot of color that no one could ever confuse with a funeral arrangement.

She felt Ethan's fingers tighten around hers, and she realized that they were still holding hands, had been ever since the veterinarian had begun to examine poor Daisy. Sloane let Ethan guide her out of the bright room. She stood beside him while he recited his cell number to the receptionist. She waited with him while a bored barista served up two cups of coffee—a dark roast for Ethan, decaf for her. She watched as he doctored her cup, adding a healthy dose of cream, stirring in a single packet of sugar.

She roused herself enough to carry her own cup to the table, and she was vaguely conscious of Ethan holding her chair for her, waiting to make sure that she was settled before he folded himself into his own seat. Reflexively, she started to drink, but the beverage was still too hot. Nevertheless, Ethan managed to swallow his.

She waited until he'd returned the paper cup to the table before she finally asked, "What are we going to do?"

"Let's wait until we hear what the doctor has to say."

"Grade five," she said, finally getting to the question she'd been unable to choke out back in the examining room. "That's serious, isn't it?"

She saw the discomfort on his face and realized that he wanted to duck the truth, to lie to her. She also recognized the moment that he decided to face the problem head-on, the moment that he embraced the first word on her list. Truth. "Yes," he said. "It's serious."

"What will happen?" She could see that he longed to avoid responding, that he was going to tell her to wait for Dr. Johnson's report. She pushed urgency into her voice. "Assuming the worst. Assuming that all the tests come out wrong."

"We might be able to treat her with drugs. She'll probably have a shortened life, depending on what the underlying cause is."

He ticked off the possibilities, falling back on his medical training. He wasn't a veterinarian, of course, but he'd seen enough lab results based on animal studies. Treatment options spread in front of them like some sort of strange tree. Dr. Johnson would report back with specific information, which would open up new courses of action. They'd make a decision, shutting off some possibilities, opening up others.

Cold. Mechanical. Manageable.

He saw the way his tone was affecting Sloane. She curled into herself. She probably wasn't even aware that she spread her fingers across her belly again, as if she were protecting their child, shielding their baby from bad news about the puppy.

He should reach out to her. He should take her hand, offer whatever comfort he could. He should tell her that they'd make it through this, no matter what happened, no matter what the doctor said.

But he'd fought too hard to build a wall around himself, to protect himself from ever having to say words like that, to anyone, under any circumstances. Not after what he'd seen his parents go through. Not after losing first his sister, then his brother. He'd only been a child himself, but he still remembered the pain.

Damn Zach and his idiotic silent auction! Who gave away puppies in a ballet fundraiser, anyway? And what sort of breeder ended up with puppies this sick? He'd sue the breeder. File an action before sunset tonight. Make

Zach draw up the papers—otherwise, what good was it to have a lawyer for a best friend?

He reached for his phone, but he was distracted by Sloane taking a sip of her coffee. She set the cup down with absolute precision, as if moving carefully would earn her precious "good girl" points, something she could cash in for a miracle.

He sighed. He'd have time to sic Zach on the breeder later. For now, he owed it to Sloane to be present for her. To help her through whatever was going to happen. He forced his tone to be light as he asked, "Did you have any pets when you were growing up?"

Sloane heard the question, felt it pull her back from the whirlpool of despairing thoughts that threatened to carry her away. *Don't borrow trouble,* she reminded herself. *Just wait until you know what's actually going on.* She tried to picture some of the bright drawings in the Hope Project, the smiling suns and giant tempera flowers that children painted when they were happy. When they were safe.

"A few," she answered Ethan, forcing herself to take a deep, steadying breath. "When I was in fourth grade, my foster family had a goose."

"A goose!"

She'd surprised him with that. The thought made her smile, despite her worry about Daisy. "It lived in a screened-in porch, on the side of the house. It was huge—its beak came up to my chest, when it straightened its neck. It was better than any watchdog. It would make a racket if anyone even drove up the driveway."

"What do you feed a goose? Goose chow?"

She laughed at his incredulous expression. "Cracked corn. Weeds from the garden. Some canned cat food, for protein. The family had owned Gertrude since she was a gosling."

"Gertrude? You're pulling my leg!"

"I'm not! Scout's honor!" She raised three fingers, as if she were taking some solemn vow. "I was terrified of her when I first got there. She would hiss whenever she got excited, and she'd flap her wings around. After a while, though, we sort of became friends. I'd talk to her every night. Tell her about my day at school, about all the cute boys I liked."

"Cute boys, hmm?" He gave her a mock-ferocious glare. "Anyone I need to worry about?"

"I don't think Billy Burton is going to ask me to the school dance any time soon."

"He might," Ethan pushed.

"Last I heard, Billy was married to his high school sweetheart, and they had four children—two sets of twins."

"Sounds like the man might want to get away from all that," Ethan growled. "Maybe I should get a goose or two, to make sure he stays off my property."

Sloane laughed despite herself. It felt good to hear Ethan teasing her. Good to hear his possessiveness. No one had ever fought for her before, not even in jest. "What about you?" she asked. "What pets did you have?"

His lips twisted into a wry smile. "Grandmother isn't exactly a 'pet' type of woman."

"What does that mean?"

"She wasn't about to let an animal track dirt into her home. It was bad enough having an unruly boy around. Besides—" he ratcheted his voice into a falsetto that was obviously supposed to represent his grandmother's speech "—no housekeeper could possibly be expected to keep up with the fur a dog or cat would shed."

"You poor thing," Sloane said, reacting more to the child he had been than the man who sat across from her now.

His hazel eyes glinted as he took another sip of coffee. "You understand, then. I had no choice but to bring home a snake."

"A snake!"

It was harmless, an albino corn snake," he said, and she could hear the remnants of the enthusiasm he must have felt as a boy. "I set it up in a terrarium, with a heat lamp and a rock. I fed it a live mouse once a week."

"That's terrible!"

"Only for the mouse," he said, pinching his fingers together as if he held a tiny rodent. He shook the make-believe creature in front of her, and she couldn't help but cringe, laughing all the while. He dropped the imaginary mouse, twisting his fingers to grab her wrist, to pull her closer to him. His lips were surprisingly soft against hers, and she found herself leaning closer, wanting more, needing some solid reassurance as she was capsized by another wave of worry about Daisy. He cupped her cheek with his palm, and she leaned against his smooth skin, closing her eyes to take a steadying breath.

"Ethan," she said, back to asking herself the questions she knew he wouldn't answer.

He said, "We're great caretakers for a puppy, aren't we? With only a goose and a snake between us, for past experience?"

"We can learn," she said. Suddenly, her response seemed unbearably important, much more relevant than any single thought about any single little dog. "We can always learn."

His eyes darkened, but he didn't have a chance to respond because his phone rang. She leaped back in her chair, as if she'd been bitten by his harmless albino corn snake.

Ethan answered before the ring was complete. "Hartwell," he snapped. "Yes. Fine. We'll be right there." He terminated the call and started to collect their cups, not meeting her eyes.

"Ethan?" she asked.

"Let's go."

He held the doors for her, the one leading out of the coffee shop, the one going into the vet's office. But she felt him pull away emotionally. She knew that if she reached for his hand, it wouldn't be there. Her fingers would twine around empty air.

Dr. Johnson was waiting for them in the examining room. She'd clipped X-rays onto a light box, and she'd spread out an array of papers on the table—medical charts, spiky test results that clearly detailed heart function.

Daisy was overjoyed to see Sloane and Ethan. The puppy yipped a greeting, then danced onto her hind paws, begging to be cuddled. Sloane gathered up the animal automatically, burying her face in the dog's black-and-white curls. She heard Ethan demand a full report, and Dr. Johnson responded like a battlefield medic.

Stage 5 heart murmur. Cardiomyopathy. Breed prone to the disease. Medication. Shortened life expectancy.

The words flowed over Sloane, sweeping her aside like eddies on a dangerous river. She caught a sob at the back of her throat, managing a strangled hiccup that made Daisy tilt her head to one side in adorable confusion. Sloane scratched the sweet dog's neck and cut off some technical question that Ethan was posing, some request for obscure medical details. "Is she in any pain?"

The vet turned to her with a sympathetic smile. "No. She'll get fatigued earlier than a healthy dog would. She may develop a cough. Of course, you won't be able to breed her."

"But it isn't cruel to keep her with us? To keep her alive?" Sloane's voice broke on the last word, but she forced herself to look directly in the doctor's eyes.

"Not at all. You should have a few good years with her, given proper medication, and adapting to her needs for a relatively quiet life."

That was all Sloane needed to hear. She let Ethan ask his questions, then, technical things about the chambers of the heart, blood tests, biochemical profiles. She heard the answers, understood them, but they didn't matter. Not for now. Not when she knew that she could have some real time to enjoy Daisy's companionship.

Ethan nodded as the doctor finished her explanation. He requested a complete copy of the medical file, including the X-rays. He'd have everything reviewed by one of his own veterinarians, by one of his trusted Hartwell Genetics staff, but he had no reason to doubt what Dr. Johnson was saying.

He shook the vet's hand, thanking her for giving them so much of her time. He watched Sloane gather up the puppy, cuddling the thing against her chest as they headed out. He produced his credit card without thinking, signed the receipt automatically. It was second nature to hold the door for Sloane, to open the back of the SUV, to work the latch on the dog's crate.

The animal turned three instinctive circles before she collapsed on the soft bedding, sighing as if she'd had a thoroughly satisfying outing. Sloane laughed and chucked the dog under her chin, and then Ethan secured the latch, tugging twice to make sure the animal was safe. He opened Sloane's door, waited for her to settle, closed the door and headed for the driver's seat.

He was already composing an email to Zach. If Ethan were able to act alone, he would insist on the breeder taking back the damaged animal. Let someone else be responsible for the rest of this miserable story. But one look at Sloane made him certain that she would never accept that action.

He was stuck with a creature that was doomed to die well before its rightful time. And there was nothing he could do about it. Nothing at all. Except refuse to be taken in. Refuse to get attached. Refuse to get anymore involved than he already was.

Ethan turned the key in the ignition, closing his ears to Sloane's crooning as she comforted her puppy on the short drive home.

Chapter Six

Two and a half weeks later, Sloane sat in another medical office, glancing uneasily at the clock. Dr. Phillip Morton was running late—half an hour so far. Of course, he was an obstetrician, and he couldn't control emergencies that came up among his pregnant patients.

Sloane glanced down at the forms she had completed, the endless pages that asked for shockingly personal information. It always bothered her to fill out medical documents. She had so little information about her parents, no real family history to include. Most doctors looked at her with suspicion when they saw how many questions she left blank. She never got used to that pause before she could explain, before she could say, "I didn't know my father, and I only have limited information about my mother."

At least Ethan had taken over for some of the forms. He had filled in all the blanks that related to insurance, to money, to the cost of the medical care she was about to receive. He completed his own profile as well, dashing off information about his personal health, diseases that ran in his family. He filled in the box labeled "other," recording details about the genetic anomaly that underlay this entire office visit.

She'd half expected him to leave as soon as the paperwork was complete. He had delivered his insurance card to the front desk, though, and then he'd sat beside her. His keys jangled in his pocket as he settled into his chair. He'd insisted on driving them to the doctor's office, powering his own luxury car through the crowded city streets and giving his driver the morning off.

Sloane was just grateful that they hadn't taken the SUV. She would always associate that vehicle with Dr. Johnson, with Daisy, with the sad news about the puppy's cardiomyopathy. Not that the little dog seemed to understand anything about her illness. The Old English sheepdog had taken to jumping up on Sloane's lap whenever she could, curling up as if she were a lapdog. Daisy was putting on weight every day. Between the puppy's size and Sloane's own expanding waistline, the practice couldn't continue, but it was certainly fun while it lasted.

Not that Ethan had even noticed. He now ignored Daisy whenever he could, acting as if the sweet little animal was invisible. He no longer scratched behind her ears, and he'd stopped taking her for walks. Come to think of it, Sloane couldn't even remember the last time he'd referred to the dog by name.

Sloane wasn't a fool. She knew what he was doing. He was protecting himself, keeping his heart safe from future pain. But he was also missing out on all the fun and joy that Daisy could give them—potential years of canine love and affection.

Sloane glanced at Ethan, wondering if she dared raise the issue while they waited. He was stunning in his navy suit, the fabric offset with the faintest pinstripe. His shirt was bright white, almost blinding across his chest, at his wrists. He wore a conservative burgundy tie, perfectly knotted, as if he were expecting to be photographed at any minute.

Which, if the press ever found out what they were doing that morning, would certainly be the case.

Her belly churned with anxiety. She wanted to stand up, to pace across the room, to work off some of the nervous energy that sparked through her body. Instead, she recrossed her legs. There was nothing to do but wait.

She clenched her hands in her lap, rubbing her right thumb against her left palm. She'd never imagined that she'd be sitting here in the office of one of the world's foremost obstetricians, waiting for a test that could dictate the entire future of her life.

Not that anything would change. She was going to keep this baby no matter what the test results showed, even if they confirmed the worst possible news, the strongest form of the Hartwell genetic curse.

She almost wished that she was innocent again, that she still believed that the amnio was only necessary to prove that Ethan was the father of her child. Then she could have believed that everything would work out perfectly. One quick medical confirmation of a fact she knew could never be in doubt, and all would be settled.

But in reality, everything was tangled. Everything was confused. Three weeks ago, at Ethan's insistence, Sloane had phoned her landlord and told him that she was breaking her lease. She'd agreed to have her furniture donated; she didn't even know where it had been sent. James had taken care of that. James had taken care of everything, dispatching movers to collect one more suitcase of clothes, her favorite coffee mug, a handful of trinkets.

Two medium-size boxes. That was all she owned. If today's test came back with devastating news, and she took the stand she knew she had to take, Ethan might very well throw her out of his house. She could put all of her belongings into the trunk of a taxi. But where would she tell the driver to take her?

She closed her eyes and leaned her head back against the wall. She was just nervous about the procedure. Everything was going to be fine. Even if the amnio revealed Ethan's worst fears, he wasn't going to kick her out. She had to believe that.

"Are you all right?" His voice was low, vibrating with an edge of concern she'd never heard before.

Her eyes fluttered open. "I'm fine. Just nervous."

"The procedure isn't supposed to hurt."

She managed a wry smile. "That's what all the fathers say."

His face shuttered closed, and he shifted in his seat, increasing the gulf between them. Before she could think of something to tell him, something to smooth over the awkward silence, a nurse appeared across the waiting room. "Ms. Davenport?"

Sloane grabbed a deep breath and got to her feet. She took two steps before she turned back to Ethan, ready to tell him that he should feel free to take a walk, to get out of the waiting room, that he should just go into his office, and she would call a cab to take her home.

He was right behind her, so close, in fact, that he reached out a hand to steady her, to keep her from falling backward. His fingers on her arm were cold, like granite.

"I—" she said, flustered.

"I'm coming with you."

There was no way to argue with the grim determination on his face. She swallowed and turned back to the waiting nurse, trying to pretend that Ethan was always by her side, that he was always her companion. That she had no doubt they would stay that way for years and years to come. *Partnership,* she thought grimly. She was the one who had put the word on that damned piece of paper.

Ethan barely noticed the hall they walked down. The procedure room was the same as thousands he'd seen before, the same as all the other offices where Hartwell Genetics worked its magic. An examining table covered with fresh white paper. A chair. A hanger on the back of the door. An ultrasound machine, lights already blinking to show that it was ready to serve. The nurse delivered her standard patter, handing Sloane a paper gown, telling her to leave it open at the front, departing with an efficient swirl of papers.

All too soon, the two of them were alone, and Sloane had donned the flimsy paper garment.

He could see that she was terrified. She was putting on a brave face, pretending that nothing would go wrong, but he could read her tension in the set of her jaw, in the line of her lips as she swallowed noisily.

His palms itched. He wanted to close the distance between them. He wanted to kiss those pale lips, whisper against her cheek that everything was going to be fine, that he would be there for her, no matter what the tests revealed.

He couldn't do that, though. He couldn't make a promise that he wasn't certain he could keep.

He was spared the need to drum up small talk by a sharp knock on the door. Sloane jumped as much as he did before the door opened and Phillip Morton glided into the room.

"Phil," Ethan said, smoothly stepping forward and extending his hand.

"Ethan."

Phil was an old business colleague. They had sat on advisory boards together, played more than a few rounds of golf. Ethan had chosen Phil because he knew the man had impeccable credentials and hands-on experience to match the sterling diplomas on his wall. More than that, though, Phil knew the Hartwell family history. He understood the science behind Ethan's greatest fear.

The obstetrician reached out to shake Sloane's hand, offering her a professional smile, automatic reassurances. The nurse returned to assist with the procedure, and Ethan moved to the far side of the examining table, trying to stay out of the way.

Sloane had grown stoic. Her nerves were more apparent now. She fiddled with that ridiculous paper gown, tracing her fingers back and forth along one edge. She answered Phil's questions with as few words as possible, her voice pitched half an octave higher than usual. Several times, she took deep, isolated breaths, as if she were reminding herself to fill her lungs, to exhale her fear, to relax as best she could.

Soon enough, she was reclining on the table. Her eyes widened in alarm as the nurse applied gel to her belly, preparing her for the ultrasound that would guide the doctor's needle. Sloane swallowed, the sound clearly audible in the sterile room. For the first time, Ethan could see the gentle swell of her changed body, the soft curve that told him that there really was a baby, that there really was a new life that they'd created.

He couldn't do this for her, couldn't place his own body on the table instead of hers. But he could help her. He could do his best to ease her fear.

Snagging a chair with his wingtip-clad foot, he sat down close to her head. With one hand, he reached out to smooth a stray lock of hair from her cheek. With the other, he captured her own hand, twining his fingers between hers.

She turned to look at him, tears filming the saturated blue of her eyes. "It's okay," he whispered, leaning down to place his lips against the shell of her ear. A rush of tenderness threatened to close his throat, and his voice grew rough as he said, "Everything is going to be fine."

The words were a prayer for him, an invocation for everything that was good and bright and kind within the universe to preserve him, to keep him from being a liar, now, when the words were the most important he'd ever uttered in his life. He passed his free palm over Sloane's forehead, trying to soothe away the worried lines he found there. "Relax," he said. "It's almost over."

Phil nodded in approval as Ethan spoke. The doctor's hands moved smoothly, with the ease of familiarity. He narrated his actions, letting Sloane prepare for the slight pinch as he inserted his needle, telling her that everything was going as expected, that everything was routine.

Soon enough, they were done. Sloane heard Dr. Morton's patter. She felt the nurse wipe away the ultrasound gel. She understood that she was supposed to wait for fifteen minutes, then sit up, get dressed, meet Dr. Morton in his office down the hall. The door to the examining room closed.

"Ethan," she whispered, turning her head to see him.

"Thank you," he responded in the same subdued tone. "I'm sorry." He lifted her hand, the one that was still wrapped inside his stony fingers. His lips across its back were dry, nearly weightless, like a memory of autumn leaves.

He lowered his head to her shoulder.

Sloane wanted to stroke the golden strands of his hair, wanted to tell him that everything was going to be fine, that he had no reason to apologize, that he hadn't done anything bad or evil or cruel. She knew he wouldn't listen, though, knew he wouldn't believe her. She stared up at the ceiling instead, reminding herself to take deep breaths, waiting until it was safe for her to stand, to get dressed, to carry on as if nothing whatsoever had happened.

Dr. Morton was waiting for them in his office, a veritable forest of mahogany and brass, with deep leather chairs that looked like they belonged in an antique boardroom. "We'll have results in ten days," he said.

Ethan cleared his throat. "Surely you can expedite this."

Dr. Morton shook his head. "Some tests take time to run, Ethan. We can't rush nature." There was a mild sharpness to the doctor's tone, a hint of rebuke. That sting, though, was gone when Dr. Morton returned his gaze to Sloane. "Take it easy for the rest of the day. Stay off your feet as much as possible. Drink plenty of fluids. No sex for twenty-four hours."

Sloane studiously avoided looking at Ethan. No sex for a lot longer than that. Not until after they were truly married.

Dr. Morton shook their hands as they stood to leave. He spared a grave smile for Sloane. "Ms. Davenport, please don't hesitate to phone me if you have any questions. Any questions at all."

"Thank you," she said, liking his solemn sincerity. Ethan had been right. Transferring her care to Dr. Morton was a good thing. It was a tremendous comfort to know that she could schedule her monthly appointments, that she could follow through on everything that was good for the baby.

Ethan held the door for her as they left the office. He wished that he could do more, that he could make the next ten days disappear, that he could write a check, empty a bank account, open a vein to guarantee the results he craved.

Instead, he was reduced to idiotic, everyday tasks. He insisted on pulling the car around to the elevator lobby so that Sloane wouldn't have to walk even the short distance through the parking lot. He opened the door for her and hovered a protective hand above her head as she gracefully eased herself onto the seat. He barely resisted the urge to lean across, to tug at her seat belt to make sure that she had secured it properly.

Once he was back in the driver's seat, he double-checked his mirrors. He made his way through the streets like a model citizen, observing every speed limit, gliding to a perfect stop at every red light. He felt as if he were making a bargain with heaven, that he was offering up his good behavior in exchange for his dreams.

As he helped her out of the car, he caught a whiff of her scent, the honeysuckle freshness that always surrounded her. Unconsciously, he braced himself for the tug in his groin, for the hot lance of lust that she awakened in him without any effort at all. Instead, he felt a throbbing ache in his chest, a terrifying surge that nearly stopped his heart.

She was so brave. So determined. So willing to sacrifice for him, for their child.

He only hoped that he had not betrayed her, that his genes had not paved the path for the destruction of everything good that was growing between them.

Inside the house, he trailed after her, up the stairs to the guest suite. Feeling like a stranger in his own home, he glided over to her bed. The comforter felt foreign beneath his fingers; he might never have seen it before. The sheets were crisp, clean, but they held no familiarity, no saucy temptation of heat, of memory, of passion. He folded them back as if he were completing a ritual, a prayer.

Ethan's navy suit was incongruous as he worked; he stood out like a preacher at a motel. A strangely luxurious motel, but a motel all the same. Only when he'd run out of things to do, when he'd finished all the business of seeing to her comfort did he actually meet her eyes.

"Ten days," she said, betraying the thought that had nagged at her all the way home.

"And then we'll know." He raised his hand, settled his chilly palm against her cheek. A shudder crinkled down her spine, even as she turned her head to lean against his fingers. "Get some rest," he whispered. "I'll have James bring you some lunch."

"Ethan? Will you bring Daisy up here? I'd like to have her beside me while I sleep."

His shoulders stiffened, and she knew that he wanted to refuse. He didn't want anything to do with the puppy, with a living, breathing reminder that genetic mishaps did occur. She knew that she needed to talk to him, needed to tell him that he was wrong to ignore the dog.

But she couldn't. Not right then. Not when she was so tired that she could barely keep her eyes open.

Ethan's voice was gravely courteous as he said, "I'll have James take care of that."

That. A living, breathing puppy was reduced to "that." Sloane swallowed hard, and Ethan ducked out the door before she could make any verbal response.

As soon as he was gone, Sloane slipped out of her summer sundress. She'd gone on the shopping spree that Ethan had recommended. New clothes hung in her closet, spanning the range from casual to formal. Her dresser drawers were filled with satin and lace; she had splurged on intriguing lingerie that had made her blush even as she imagined what Ethan would say when he finally saw it.

For now, though, she dug to the back of the drawer, shoving aside garments that still bore their price tags. Her fingers closed on her old cotton nightgown, and the softness of the fabric nearly brought tears to her eyes. She shrugged it over her bare shoulders, relishing the familiar feel. She yawned as she climbed into bed. The morning had been so emotionally fraught, so charged, that she felt as if she'd run a marathon. She was asleep before James arrived with his tray. His tray, and Daisy.

Once Ethan was certain that Sloane was sleeping soundly, he headed for his office. He knew that James would call him if anything went wrong, if there was anything at all that he could do back at the house.

Watching Sloane's grim determination that morning had made him realize that he was long overdue in attending to his own difficult matters. It was time to confront his grandmother, time to declare that he was marrying Sloane Davenport.

Of course, there was the usual rigmarole in the waiting area outside his grandmother's office suite. The grim-faced secretary waved him to a seat, treating him like he was some unwelcome petitioner. Well, Ethan wasn't going to put up with that. Not today. Not when he had such an important message to deliver.

Ignoring the squawk of professional outrage from the secretary, Ethan marched straight into the lion's den.

Grandmother was on the phone, nodding her head at something that was being said on the other end of the line. She took one look at Ethan's face, though, and she interrupted whoever was talking. "I'm sorry, Richard. Something has come up here. I'll call you back later." She hung up the phone without waiting for a response, as if she were an actress in a movie. "Ethan," she said levelly.

"Grandmother."

The trip to Paris had not been as beneficial as he had hoped. Dark circles still stood out beneath the hazel eyes that matched his own. Grandmother's cheeks were still pale, and he couldn't help but dart a glance to her hands, taking quick measure of the tremor there. As if she knew exactly what he was doing, she folded her fingers into her palms, drawing herself up to her fullest height. "I tried to reach you in your office this morning," she said. "I wanted to discuss the supply figures from Singapore."

"I was out," he said. "At Philip Morton's office." He saw the flash of recognition in his grandmother's eyes, the instant that she registered the name of the prominent obstetrician.

"I assume from your tone that you had a personal reason for being there? Not some study you're asking him to conduct for the company?"

His tone. Ethan had been accused of using the wrong

tone ever since he was a child. Well, he was long past
the age where he would roll his eyes and click his tongue
in teenage exasperation. Instead, he harnessed all of his
skills as a successful business executive, every lesson
he'd ever learned about meaningful communication,
about driving home his personal agenda in a dog-eat-
dog world.

Because there was nothing more personal than his
relationship with Sloane Davenport.

"Grandmother, you told me that you wanted me married by January. I'll meet your deadline, with a couple
of months to spare."

There. He'd caught her by surprise.

But it only took a moment for her to follow his words
to their logical conclusion, from Philip Morton to her
damnable birthday ultimatum. "So, you got a girl in the
family way, and now you're going to marry her. Is she
one of your actresses? Or is she a model?"

He shook his head, resisting the urge to protest the
way she always thought the worst of him. Then again,
he hadn't given her a lot of reason to think otherwise,
not where his personal life was concerned. "Her name
is Sloane Davenport. We met at the AFAA auction. She
used to work for the foundation."

"Used to? Where does she work now?"

He hedged his answer, knowing precisely how his
grandmother would interpret the unvarnished truth of
Sloane's unemployment. "She's a freelancer, working
in the area of child psychology."

"Ethan." She turned his name into an essay of warning. "What do you really know about this woman?"

He bristled at the implied accusation. "I know that
she's no gold digger, Grandmother. She's not staying

with me because she expects a share of the Hartwell fortune, if that's what you're worried about."

"And the baby?" Grandmother sounded like a particularly troublesome shareholder in the midst of an annual meeting. "Does she know about the risk?"

What kind of man did his grandmother think he was? "Of course she knows. That's why we were at Phil's office this morning. We'll have the test results in ten days."

"And will she stick around if the results are bad?"

"Grandmother—"

"I'm just asking, Ethan. You're talking about spending the rest of your life with this woman, and I want to know if she has what it takes to handle bad news. The worst."

His own parents hadn't. They'd abandoned him when the going got tough. Sloane was different, though. She was more determined than Ethan was himself. He knew that, even though it frightened him to admit it. "She'll stay with me, Grandmother. No matter what the test shows."

"Very well," Grandmother said after a long pause. She nodded as if they'd just decided to change the color of their corporate logo. "You'll bring her to the *No Comment,* on Independence Day?"

Grandmother's yacht. Site of her annual Fourth of July party, where scores of friends and business associates would gather for the finest catered foods and the best view of fireworks over the Potomac River.

"Of course," he said. "There's nothing we'd like more."

She didn't bother to call him on the lie. Instead, she let him turn on his heel, let him cross all the way to the office door. As he settled his hand on the knob, though, she called out his name. "Ethan, I have to warn you. If

I find this girl wanting, if I think that she's only trying to use you for your name or your money, I'll follow through on my original plan. I can still step down from the board and donate all my shares to AFAA."

He turned back to meet her gaze, hazel eyes to hazel. "Of course you can, Grandmother. You'll do whatever you have to do. Sloane and I will see you on the Fourth."

He left before she could get in the last word.

Chapter Seven

Ethan told himself that he didn't need to worry. He'd attended Independence Day celebrations on the *No Comment* for years. He was used to his grandmother's sly power plays, to the barbed comments she made, all in the name of family love. This year wouldn't be any different.

Except it was. This year, Sloane was with him.

She looked stunning as she stood at the boat's railing, the picture of health in a bright blue sundress. He had no idea what sort of fabric that thing was, or how a designer would describe the cut. All he could say was that the color set off the glow of her eyes, made her hair seem even darker in the brilliant late-afternoon sun. He came up beside her, handing over a glass of sparkling water before he leaned against the railing. "Compliments of the *No Comment*," he said.

She flashed a smile at him. "I've never been on a boat large enough to have a 'below.'"

"I'm sure Grandmother would love to show you around. Just brace yourself to answer a thousand questions in payment for the privilege."

She gave him a concerned look. "Maybe we shouldn't have come, if you feel so strongly about her."

He just shook his head. There was a lot that Sloane had to learn about the Hartwell family. A lot that he should tell her. But not yet. Not now. Not while they were still waiting for news about the amnio, about the baby's health. There'd be time enough to give her the full background on Grandmother and the old woman's ridiculous, controlling demands.

He smiled to ease the frown that was starting to settle onto Sloane's lips. "You need to meet each other, and there's no time like the present. I just wish that we didn't have to stay on this boat until the fireworks display ends. There are better ways to spend a summer evening."

She quickly took a swallow of her drink in a fruitless attempt to tame the blush that leaped to her cheeks. Over the past month, Ethan had scrupulously honored their agreement; he'd never come close to pushing her beyond her comfort zone, sexually. He certainly wasted no time, though, teasing her, alluding to the things that he would do once her ban on bedroom play was lifted. Even now, he stared at her with an amused hazel gaze, taking careful note of the way she settled her ice-filled glass against the hot pulse point in her wrist. "Let's go downstairs," he said. When she raised her chin in surprise at his proposal, he laughed. "Grandmother is down there. She'll hold court in the air-conditioning, until the sun sets."

"Well," she said, trying to muster the composure that she knew he could destroy with a single wicked glance. "I wouldn't want her to think I was afraid of her."

"Oh, she'll never think that," Ethan said.

He slipped his fingers between hers easily, holding her hand as if they'd known each other for years. Sloane looked around, surprised to realize that so many people had joined them on the yacht's deck. There must be thirty altogether, gathered in clusters of three and four. Sloane tilted her head back to look at the raised deck, where the captain was just beginning to maneuver the *No Comment* out of the marina.

"Ethan!" a voice called out. Sloane turned around to find Zach Crosby approaching. The two men shook hands, and Zach leaned in to settle a quick kiss on Sloane's cheek. "I'm glad that both of you could make it," Zach said, directing a concerned glance at Sloane. "Ethan said you weren't feeling well earlier this week?"

She resisted the urge to settle a protective hand over her belly. Instead, she smiled at the honest worry on the man's face. No reason to fill him in on the amnio test, on the nerve-jangling wait for results. "I'm fine, now."

"Ethan told me about Daisy. I was so sorry to hear about her condition. I certainly never intended to cause any problems for you."

Sloane made herself smile again, hoping to ease the earnest frown on Zach's face. "*You* didn't cause the problems. Sometimes these things just happen. No one's to blame." She glanced at Ethan, hoping that he'd say something to smooth things over. He didn't oblige, and she fought the urge to chide him.

At least Zach seemed to miss the momentary tension between them. "Thanks for your understanding," he said. "Hey, did Ethan tell you about the Fourth of July when we brought firecrackers on board the *No Comment?* We were thirteen, and we thought we were in charge of the universe."

She laughed at the energy in Zach's voice, at the image of two mischievous boys, wreaking havoc on the boat's deck. "I think he forgot to mention that one."

"Zach—" Ethan warned, but there was no deterring his best friend.

"Ethan bought them in the first place, but it was my idea to bring them on board."

"I don't think Sloane wants to hear—" Ethan started to complain, but there was resigned laughter behind his words.

"Oh, no," Sloane protested. "I'm very interested in this. Go on, Zach. Tell me more."

"Ethan figured out how to rig them under the starboard railing. He wanted to see what would happen if all the guests ran to one side of the boat at the same time."

"It was a study in physics," Ethan said piously. "Newton's third law. Every action causes an equal and opposite reaction."

"That's not what your grandmother said when she caught us."

"My grandmother didn't appreciate the finer points of the scientific method."

Zach's eyes sparkled. "She appreciated free labor, in any case. It took us three whole days of summer vacation to scrub down the deck after the party. The worst part, though, was that she insisted on checking our pockets for the next three years, whenever we got anywhere near the boat."

Sloane was pleased to hear Ethan laugh at the memory. To hear him talk about his childhood, there had been so much that was dark, so much pain. It was a revelation to discover that Ethan actually had some good memories.

"What do you think of Margaret?" Zach asked Sloane.

"Actually, I haven't really met her yet. Just shaken her hand at the AFAA gala and thanked her for coming. I'm sure she doesn't remember me at all."

Ethan said, "We were just heading below."

Zach nodded, directing a warning to Sloane. "Don't believe everything he tells you. Margaret Hartwell isn't really a tyrant. It's been years since she had anyone flogged on board the *No Comment.*"

"Enough!" Ethan exclaimed in mock exasperation, and then he said to Sloane, "Shall we?" He settled a hand on her hip and pulled her away with a tantalizing hint of possession.

He glanced quickly at Sloane before he led the way down the stairs. She'd had the good sense to wear flat sandals—no chance that she'd lose her footing on the narrow steps. Nevertheless, he felt anxious each time she settled her feet. He wished that he could gather her into his arms, that he could carry her through the passage ahead. Of course, if his hands were anywhere near her bare flesh, he and Sloane might not make it as far as Grandmother's sitting room. He just might wander into one of the bedrooms, by "mistake."

The stairs negotiated, Sloane came to stand beside him. They entered the dragon's lair together.

As he had expected, Margaret Hartwell was sitting on her favorite throne, the massive armchair that faced the doorway of the elegantly appointed room. She must have come fresh from the hairdresser that morning; he could still smell the hairspray that held her white aura in place. She wore a classic summer suit, all in navy. Her fingernails were painted the same orange-red that she'd worn forever, perfectly applied and a single shade too bright.

"Ethan, dear," she said, tilting her face for him to kiss. He was pleased to see some color in her face, and she looked a little less fatigued than she had earlier in the week.

"Grandmother." He brushed his lips against her cheek. "May I present Sloane Davenport? Sloane, this is my grandmother, Margaret Hartwell."

He brought Sloane forward, fighting the urge to roll his eyes at his grandmother's formality, at her turning a simple meeting into an audience with a queen.

For one insane moment, Sloane wondered if she was supposed to curtsy. There was something about the awkward way Ethan was holding himself, the stiffness that jammed his spine, that turned him into a man she'd never seen before.

Margaret, though, offered her hand and a smile, the very image of a perfect hostess. "Sloane, dear. How very nice to meet you. I must say, you look very familiar to me…"

Sloane hoped that her own fingers weren't trembling too much as she shook hands. "We've met before, very briefly. At the AFAA Spring Gala."

"Of course!" Mrs. Hartwell exclaimed. "Ethan told me that you are no longer with the foundation. He said that you're doing something related to…child psychology?"

Sloane flashed an uncertain glance at Ethan. How much had he told Mrs. Hartwell about Sloane's ignominious dismissal from the woman's pet charity? She tried to sound confident as she said, "I'm developing a computerized art therapy system, to help children adjust to foster care."

Margaret nodded with something that looked like approval. "That sounds quite complicated."

"It is," Sloane said, "but there's a real need out there."

"I would love to hear more about your work. Have you looked into market distribution, anything like that?"

Ethan finally stepped forward, shattering his own awkward stance with an exasperated sigh. "Grandmother, we didn't come here expecting to be grilled by a venture capitalist."

"I don't mind—" Sloane started to say, but Mrs. Hartwell cut her off.

"You're quite right, Ethan. We shouldn't mix business with pleasure. Could you be a dear and get me a drink? A gin and tonic with—"

"Extra ice and three limes." Sloane heard the bored familiarity in Ethan's tone, and she expected him to smile indulgently. His face was grim, though, and he hesitated before heading over to the stairs. Sloane nodded at him, trying to convey that she would be fine, that she could handle further chat with the woman who was going to be her…grandmother-in-law?

As soon as Ethan was out of sight, Margaret patted the chair beside her. "Please, dear. Sit down. I imagine you're still getting tired easily? I assumed that you were well past morning sickness, or I'd never have suggested that Ethan bring you onto the *No Comment.*"

Sloane tried not to look surprised. She parsed the tone of the old woman's words, fearful that she'd hear disdain or disapproval. Neither was present, though. Just good old-fashioned solicitude for a guest. "I—thank you," she said, sitting down. "I've felt much better the past few weeks."

"I trust that my grandson is taking good care of you?"

"Of course, Mrs. Hartwell."

The old woman tsked. "Now doesn't *that* sound stuffy. And 'Grandmother' sounds like something out of a British drama, even coming from Ethan. Why don't we try 'Margaret.'"

"Margaret," Sloane said, smiling. "Yes, Margaret, Ethan has been quite kind to me."

"Kind." Margaret tilted her head to one side, like a magpie evaluating a particularly sparkly treasure. "I see that he bought you a lovely ring."

Self-conscious, Sloane extended her hand. Margaret grasped her fingers lightly, turning her wrist to get a better view. "It was such a surprise," Sloane confided. "I never expected anything so beautiful." She stopped, realizing that Margaret might interpret her words as a criticism of Ethan. "I mean, Ethan has wonderful taste. Of course, he'd choose a beautiful ring. I just meant…"

She trailed off. What was she going to say? Her engagement to Ethan had been a business arrangement? A way for both of them to provide for the well-being of their child, the baby that neither of them had anticipated on that breath-stealing night at the Eastern?

No. Margaret definitely did *not* need to know anything about the Eastern.

The old woman released her hand. "My grandson seems quite taken with you, dear. I hope that you won't take this the wrong way, but I've seen him with any number of women over the years, squiring them around town. He's never been quite as…attentive as he is to you. And, of course, he never actually proposed to any of the others."

Sloane heard the unspoken questions behind Margaret's statements. The older woman was honestly perplexed to find her grandson engaged. She was fishing for details. Sloane obliged by saying, "He proposed to me on the balcony of the Kennedy Center."

That wasn't quite the truth. Ethan had first proposed in the living room of her ratty basement apartment. But the proposal that mattered, the proposal that she'd *accepted,* had been at the famous landmark.

"I trust my grandson had the good sense to treat you to some romantic show first."

Sloane blushed, as if she were speaking with a girlfriend. "It was the ballet gala," she said shyly.

Margaret nodded, as if she were seeing the pieces of a jigsaw puzzle coalesce into a single coherent design. "That was Zach's event?" Sloane nodded, and Margaret said, "Poor Zach told me about the silent auction. He feels absolutely terrible about your puppy."

"He shouldn't," Sloane insisted. "Daisy is adorable, and she's doing fine, for now. We'll have some hard times ahead, but doesn't every pet owner?"

Margaret raised her eyebrows, as if Sloane had just imparted brilliant words of wisdom. "I suspect that Ethan doesn't feel quite the same way."

Before Sloane could reply, Ethan's voice came from the foot of the stairs. "Feel the same way about what?"

Ethan forced himself to keep his voice light, but he was annoyed. There'd been three people in front of him at the bar upstairs, and there hadn't been any polite way to force himself to the front of the line. He'd hated leaving Sloane alone here, hated subjecting her to one of his grandmother's famous inquisition sessions.

"Nothing, darling," Grandmother said. "We were just talking about your new puppy."

Every muscle in his body tightened. That creature was the last thing he wanted to talk about in front of Grandmother. Well, he amended, suddenly flashing on the memory of Sloane submitting to the amnio test in Philip Morton's office, the *second to last* thing. "What about it?" he asked flatly.

"Her," Sloane said.

"Excuse me?" He glanced between the two women, wondering what he was missing.

"What about *her,*" Sloane said. "Daisy isn't an *it,* she's a *her.*"

The intensity in Sloane's voice astonished him. He'd heard that tone before—when she spoke about the Hope Project—but he couldn't fathom what made her feel so strongly about the damned animal.

He glanced at Grandmother to see if she understood where Sloane's argument was coming from, and he immediately recognized the expression on her face. It was a small, wry grin, a raised-eyebrow expression that had always made him feel like he was being called on the carpet. She'd used it when he was a boy, when he was forced to face the consequences of some misbehavior, demerits or detention or some more drastic punishment. She still brought it out in business meetings, when she thought that a competitor was getting the better of him. She had leveled it against him in personal discussions, when one of his past indiscretions came home to roost.

He hated that look. And, even more, he hated the fact that Sloane was seeing it now.

He harnessed all the dispassion of his medical degree, all the cool logic that he'd learned in business school, and he said, "Her. If that's what you prefer."

Sloane bristled at the concession. Still, she might have let everything drop, if she hadn't caught the glance that Margaret shot at her. Ethan's grandmother was actually *inviting* Sloane to challenge him. Practically demanding it. And Sloane had to admit, it felt good to say, "You haven't touched that puppy since we got the diagnosis."

Ethan glared at Margaret, as if he were aware that she was some sort of instigator in this conversation. Sloane didn't care, though. This confrontation had been weeks in coming. "You think I'm an idiot for getting attached to her."

"I don't think you're an idiot!" His voice shook with some emotion. "And I don't think that we should be having this conversation here. Now." He sparked a meaningful glance toward Grandmother.

"Don't mind me," the meddlesome old woman said. Had the two of them worked this out, in the little time that he'd been upstairs? Had they banded together to force him into this?

Ethan scowled at Margaret, barely wiping the expression from his face before he turned back to Sloane. "I don't think you're an idiot," he repeated. "I just don't want you to be hurt."

"You don't get to decide that! Besides, I can't be hurt by loving something that loves me back, the way that Daisy does!"

Ethan raised his hands in a placating gesture. "You don't understand what I'm saying."

Sloane's fingers clutched at the crisp cotton that covered her belly. She raised her chin and chilled her voice until it met the temperature of Margaret's gin and tonic. "Ethan Hartwell, I understand every single word that you're saying."

It was all there. She knew that Daisy frightened him because they were ultimately going to lose her. She knew that the baby terrified him even more. The baby, and the decision that they might have to make. The decision that she would never, ever accept.

Ethan's throat worked. He started to reply to Sloane's indignant protest, seemed to decide that it was actually impossible to continue talking in front of Margaret. He stopped. Tried another approach. Stopped again. It was the first time she'd ever seen him without an easy answer, without some glib reply. At last, he gave up speaking to her at all. Instead, he glared at Margaret and said, "I hope you're happy now, Grandmother."

The old woman sighed. "No, darling. I'm not happy at all." Sloane heard the endless sorrow beneath her words—disappointment at the current situation certainly, but more than that. Sloane could only imagine how many fights there had been between the two of them, how many disagreements when a headstrong boy, now an iron-willed man, had vented his frustrations with life's unfairness.

Ethan snorted in disgust. "I don't believe that for a moment."

Sloane cut him off. "Don't you dare take this out on her!"

"She—"

"She asked a simple question," Sloane said, feeling the fragile hold she had on her own emotions start to fray. "She asked about the night you proposed to me. About the gala, and Daisy. Good things, Ethan. Nothing that *hurt*."

Ethan stared at her, hearing the frustration that she dumped on the last word. And suddenly, he realized that he should have trusted her more. He should have believed that Sloane could devote herself to Daisy, that she would be able to cope with the puppy's ultimate demise. Sloane was stronger than he'd ever given her credit for, infinitely more resilient.

"—so pleased to have made your acquaintance," she

was saying, extending her hand to his grandmother. "I'm afraid I need some fresh air."

"Dear," Grandmother started to say, but Sloane was already halfway across the room. Ethan started after her, only coming to a stop at the sword-sharp note in his grandmother's voice, calling his name.

He took his time turning around, using the pause to freeze his voice. "Yes, Grandmother."

"What were you thinking?" she said. "All these years, chasing after anything in a skirt, and you haven't learned the first thing about how a woman's mind works?"

"Sloane has nothing to do with my past, Grandmother!"

"And if you're not careful, she'll have nothing to do with your future. It's the Fourth of July, Ethan. You have six months to be married. Don't make anymore mistakes."

He started to tell her that he knew the date. He started to tell her that he hadn't made a mistake, that he'd acted in Sloane's best interest. He started to tell her that he was through with manipulation, with games.

But he couldn't waste the time. He had to find Sloane.

She had found a space on the railing, toward the back of the boat. The other guests had swarmed the luxurious buffet tables, taking advantage of the festive red, white and blue plates that encouraged everyone to indulge in gourmet picnic food. Apparently, everyone was accustomed to the notion that Margaret didn't attend her own party. Or at least that she arrived late.

Sloane didn't really care. The only thing she wanted was to get off the boat. She glanced up at the sky. The color was deepening to indigo in the east. Another fifteen minutes, maybe, before the sun actually set. An hour after that, before the fireworks were over. And yet another hour to get back to the dock.

As if she knew what she was going to do then. She certainly couldn't face going home with Ethan. Not when she had finally dared to call him on his greatest fear. Not when she had challenged him in front of his grandmother.

Maybe she could rent a hotel room downtown. As if anything would be available over the holiday weekend. She sighed and ran her fingers through her hair, suddenly feeling wilted by the July heat.

"Why don't you come sit down?" She hadn't heard Ethan come up behind her. His voice was solicitous.

"I don't want to sit down," she said. She realized that she was still angry with him. He had backed them into that impossible corner in Margaret's room, forced them into a conversation that should never have been started on board the *No Comment*.

"Come below," he whispered. "We can have some privacy there, in one of the bedrooms."

"I will *not* go into a bedroom with you!" Her voice was louder than she'd planned. She darted a look around but, mercifully, no one seemed to have heard.

Ethan sighed and shifted his weight, resting his forearms on the railing. He couldn't say anything right. He would just have to wait for Sloane to change her mind. Wait for her to get over the peak of her anger.

The guests swirled in little pockets behind them, exclaiming as they found each other in the growing twilight. Waiters passed trays of bite-size desserts, along with after-dinner drinks. Grandmother finally made her appearance, raising a round of applause and carefully orchestrated fawning by the partygoers.

Throughout it all, Ethan stood beside Sloane, locked

into her silence, riveted by her fury. The worst part of it was that she looked so beautiful. Her profile was stark against the night sky. She held her chin high. A breeze caught a few stray tendrils of her hair.

Each breath carried her unique scent to him, the combination of her delicate skin and whatever soap or perfume or fragrance she wore. In the past month, he thought he'd grown accustomed to the gentle aroma, but now he found that it awoke his own senses, heated the pads of his fingers, scratched across the back of his throat. He longed to pull her close to him, to crush the crisp fabric of her dress beneath his needy hands, to absorb her essence through his palms.

The first fireworks startled her. A quick explosion, and a spatter of crimson and white, high in the sky above them. Sloane caught a yelp at the back of her throat, even as she realized what was happening. Even as she felt Ethan tense beside her.

A dozen more blasts followed in quick succession. The concussions were nearly deafening over the river, the sound echoing back toward the shower of light. Scarlet and silver, cobalt and emerald. The guests oohed and aahed over each display, catching their collective breath in astonishment at the beauty.

Sloane tilted her head back for a better view. Her eyes filled as she watched. It was so beautiful. The entire evening could have been so beautiful, everything about it. Instead, it had all been ruined by a stupid fight. Stupid, but necessary. Because Sloane knew that she was right.

A tear snaked from the corner of her eye, trailing into her hair. She wiped at it with her palm, hurried, embarrassed. Another followed, though, and another—she couldn't stop herself from crying.

"Sloane," Ethan breathed, but she shook her head furiously.

Finally, with a grand finale that left her half-deaf, the fireworks display was over. The other guests cheered and clapped. Someone launched a chorus of "She's a Jolly Good Fellow," and Margaret made a little speech, thanking them all for joining her, exclaiming that she could never ask for more than an enjoyable night with friends and loved ones. The boat's engine finally thrummed to life, and they made their slow way back to the marina, to the dock. To freedom.

Of course, Margaret was waiting at the head of the gangplank, bidding farewell to each guest. Sloane longed to slip past her, to huddle off the boat anonymously, lost in a group of strangers. Margaret, though, made a special point of reaching for her hand, of closing her aged, knotted fingers over the sparkling diamond that had given Sloane so much pleasure only a few hours before.

"I'm sorry that we didn't have a chance to chat more, dear," Margaret said. Her voice was kind, and she waited for Sloane to meet her gaze. "I'm so glad that you came this evening."

"It was lovely," Sloane said mechanically. She was positive that Margaret was studying the remnant tracks of her tears.

Margaret reached out for her grandson's shoulders, pulling Ethan close in an awkward embrace. Sloane couldn't hear what the woman murmured, but she caught the urgency behind the words.

Ethan was astonished when his grandmother hissed, "Make this right."

"I—" he started to protest, barely remembering to keep his voice down. How could he ever have worried about Grandmother's health? She was as sturdy as an ox, pinning him with her agate eyes.

"Now," she ordered. "Make this right."

He shrugged and pulled away. Certainly Grandmother could issue her edicts. She'd been doing it her entire life. But Sloane wasn't some merger or acquisition. Sloane wasn't a government review board to be convinced about the safety and efficacy of a new treatment. Sloane wasn't an investor to be charmed into parting with millions of dollars.

Sloane was the woman he loved.

As soon as he thought the words, he knew that they were true. He should have realized it weeks before, when they had spoken together, laughed together, shared stories of their torn and tangled pasts.

It had taken arguing with her in front of Grandmother, though, hurting her in a way that he'd never intended. It had taken watching her standing at the boat's railing, pretending that she was fine, that their fight hadn't driven her to real tears....

Ethan had felt his own heart shred at her pain. They weren't playing some game, acting out some parts for Grandmother's benefit, for the investors and business partners invited to the party. This was reality. This mattered. This was life.

Sloane Davenport was the mother of his child, the woman that he loved. The woman he had hurt. And he didn't have the first clue about how to fix things.

The car was waiting for them at the end of the dock. Ordinarily, he would have been grateful for his driver, for the luxury of someone else to deal with the crowded streets, with the throng of other fireworks-viewers, everyone returning home after a long, hot summer evening. Tonight, though, Ethan regretted that he couldn't get behind the wheel of the car himself. At least driving would have given him an excuse for the unending silence between them, the jagged stillness that sucked up oxygen like a dying fire.

Why was this so difficult? Why couldn't he just talk to Sloane? After all the words they'd shared, all the conversations they'd had, why was he struck mute now?

But he knew the reason. It kept repeating inside his skull. He loved Sloane. And he had no idea how to prove that to her.

Finally, he let them into the house, working the alarm code with the ease of long familiarity. By the time he turned away from the keypad, Sloane was halfway up the stairs. He longed to follow her, but he knew that he could not. Until he found the right words, he had to let her go.

Sloane slumped against the bedroom door as soon as she had closed it.

She didn't want to be this woman. She didn't want to be so angry. So scared. So alone.

That was it. Loneliness. The loneliness of the child who had feared Angry Mother. The girl who had befriended a goose rather than figure out how to interact with human companions. The woman who had made herself so busy with school, with work, that she had never bonded to close friends. Loneliness—that was the emotion beneath all the turmoil, beneath everything else that was swirling through her head.

She shook her head and stepped out of her sensible sandals. She stripped off her dress, left it draped over the chair in front of the vanity. She added her panties, her bra. Suddenly, she was exhausted. Too tired to dig in her dresser drawers for a nightgown. Too tired to do anything but snap off the overhead light, cross the room, worm her way beneath the sheets.

As she lay naked in the darkness, she cupped her hand over her baby bump. The swell was real. She was going to have this child.

Alone.

She twisted at her engagement ring. She couldn't keep that lie on her finger. An engagement ring was a sign of trust, of promise. Ethan didn't trust her. He didn't think of her as an equal. He certainly didn't love her—he'd never come close to saying anything about love.

She couldn't wear his ring.

The stupid thing was caught on her finger. Her hands must be swollen, from the pregnancy, from standing in the heat all night. Nevertheless, she tugged harder, suddenly consumed with the notion that she had to get the platinum band off her hand. Her heart started pounding in her ears. She closed her eyes, trying to force herself to calm down.

She remembered the last time she had felt this helpless, when the reporters had confronted her on the doorstep of her sweet little apartment, the apartment that was long gone. After she left Ethan tomorrow, she would have nowhere to retreat, no place to escape to. Her lungs constricted, and her breath started to come in short, sharp pants.

It wasn't just her personal life that was ruined, either. Her professional life was going to be a wreck. She'd already lost one job because of Ethan, the AFAA. How could she move ahead with the Hope Project now? With the gossip from the past month smeared all over the internet, any potential investors would think that she was just another in a long trail of women who had ridden on Ethan's coattails, who had thrown herself into a short-lived relationship for a good time and the thrill of reading her name in the tabloids. She'd never launch Hope, never grow the website from a dream to reality.

Her heart squeezed tight, sending a spear through her chest.

Her hands curled into fists. She was having a heart attack. Here. Now. With the baby inside her, innocent and helpless. Sloane scrambled for the telephone on her nightstand. Zero. That was the only number that she needed to press. James would answer. He would help her. Save her. Her and the baby.

Her hand swung wide, knocking the bedside lamp to the floor with a crash of shattered glass. Sobbing, she fumbled for the phone again, found it, dropped it, tried to pick it up one more time.

Ethan heard the clatter from the hallway. Unable to bear the thought of exiling himself to his bedroom, he had slumped against the guest suite door. In the darkness, he'd replayed the entire disastrous night. "Make this right," Grandmother had said. Just how did she expect him to do that? How could he admit to Sloane a truth that he was nearly afraid to admit to himself?

Ethan was launching Round 731 of how his grandmother had made his life miserable when he heard the crash. Adrenaline spiked through his veins as he recognized the sound of glass breaking, the jangle of a phone smashing against the floor.

He sprang to his feet and slammed his hand against the doorknob, hurtling into the room.

His eyes were dazzled by the moonlight streaming through the window, so much more light than he'd had in the hallway. As if Sloane were illuminated from within, he could see her reaching for the nightstand, clutching her fingers over empty air. She was choking, gasping for breath, kicking against her sheets. Even as he flew across the carpet, she worked one foot free, then the other. Flailing, she cast her legs over the side of the bed, toward the sprawling phone. Toward the shattered glass.

"Sloane!" he cried, leaping onto the bed. She flowed through his arms like water, drifting away. He adjusted his grip, closed his fingers around her waist.

She fought him, her voice rising in a terrible, wordless moan. He could hear her breath stutter from her lungs, feel the heat rising off her as she writhed in panic. Flattening his palms against her hips, he pulled her back onto the bed, onto him. He folded his arms around her, pinning her hands to her sides, wrapping his legs around her, enveloping her in the fortress of his body.

"You're all right," he said. "Sloane, you're all right. Listen to me. Breathe. You're all right."

His words came to her as if she were awakening from a nightmare. She felt the iron bands of his arms holding her close against his chest. She was entwined in his legs, captured, stilled. She felt his strength against her back, his deep breaths that reminded her to take her own, to fill her lungs.

The arrow that had pierced her heart finally crumbled.

"Breathe," he said again, and she followed his instruction. "Breathe." Her chest remembered how to expand. "Breathe." She forced herself to swallow, to hold one of those deep breaths, to stop. His hands moved from her waist. He stroked the hair off her face, smoothed it back, twisted it away from her neck. "Breathe," he reminded her one last time.

"I—" she whispered, her voice broken. "I thought I was having a heart attack."

He pitched his voice to match her own, so low that she had to calm herself more to hear it. "A panic attack, more likely."

"My chest," she said.

"Do you feel any pain now?" She barely shook her head. "Numbness?" Another shake. "Tingling in your arms?" Another one. "You're going to be fine," he said.

She closed her eyes, feeling foolish. What was she doing, working herself up like that? It couldn't be good for the baby. Or for herself. And she certainly wasn't doing any favors for the bedroom. She winced. Had she really broken the lamp? And probably the phone? James was going to have a mess to deal with in the morning.

Ethan slid his arms closer around her, cradling her against his chest. Lying in the dark, listening to Sloane growing calm, Ethan knew that he had to do something, had to *say* something. *Make this right,* Grandmother had commanded.

He knew how to make business right. At Hartwell Genetics, in the office, at the helm of a Fortune 500 behemoth, Ethan knew that he had to keep information to himself. He needed to parcel out the truth, keep his employees on a need-to-know basis. He needed to outsmart his competitors, keep them in the dark about markets, about the future.

But Sloane wasn't his employee. She wasn't his competitor. She was the woman who was going to be his wife. He needed to share with Sloane. He needed to treat her as an equal. *Trust. Respect. Partnership.* She'd taught him the words weeks before, when she'd first shared her list with him.

"Sloane—" he started, but he had to stop, had to clear his throat. As much as he longed to confess everything to her, to admit his love, to tell her all the truth that he now knew, he had to apologize first. He had to make it right. "Sloane, I am so sorry. I was wrong to pull away from Daisy, to ignore her. I acted out of fear, but that is no excuse. I blocked her out of my life, and you, too. I had no right to decide how you should handle the bad news, to even try to control you that way. I am so, so sorry."

She grew absolutely still as he spoke. He felt her listening, absorbing every word. He waited for her to say something, anything.

But while he waited, his body betrayed him. His noble thoughts were cheapened by his body's realization that the most desirable woman in the world was lying, naked, in his arms. The sudden heat in his groin made him shift to relieve the pressure against the confining cloth of his trousers.

As long as he was shifting, he might as well leave the room altogether. He'd said everything that he could say. Done everything that he could do. Offered his best bid to *make it right.* She would never believe anymore words that he said, not when he'd been betrayed by a body that would never tire of Sloane's beauty.

Before he could leave the bed, though, her fingers clutched at his. Her hand folded around his, pulling him closer, keeping him near.

Sloane had felt his body stiffen; she recognized the heat of his desire, sudden and firm against her back. She knew that he was leaving in defeat, in shame.

But she also knew just how much his words had cost him, how deeply he'd been moved as he whispered to her in the darkness.

His confession hadn't come from the Ethan Hartwell of the boardroom. No. He'd spoken as the Ethan Hartwell that she'd first met in the Eastern Hotel, that she'd recognized as some sort of kindred spirit within minutes of their first words at that fateful hotel bar. This was the Ethan Hartwell who had opened his life to her.

She'd heard the remorse in his voice, heard the devastating emotion behind his confession. He was doing the best that he could. He was admitting his own fear. He was sharing, reaching out to her.

She twisted, turning to her side, letting him roll with her so that they lay on the bed, face-to-face. "I'm strong enough to do this," she said. "I'm strong enough to love Daisy. To love our baby. No matter what happens. You have to believe me. To trust me."

He brushed the hair back from her face, his fingers impossibly gentle. "I do. I understand that now." And then he knew that he could say the rest, that he *had* to say the rest, no matter how his flesh had tried to lead him astray before. "I trust you, Sloane, and I love you."

He made the words sound new, fresh, as if they'd never been spoken by any human being in the entire history of the world. Sloane might have thought that she was dazed, that she was dreaming, if she hadn't seen his lips form the syllables. Those last three words filled her, capsized her, steadied her again. She held herself perfectly still as she whispered, "I love you, too."

Only then could she lean forward to kiss him. At first, she merely brushed her lips against his. The instant that their mouths met, though, passion leaped high inside her. She parted her lips, yielded to the velvet of his tongue.

She arched her back as he ran his hand down her arm; she shivered at the heat he spread all the way to her fingertips. He raised her wrist to his lips, drank deeply of the pulse point that pounded there. "Sloane," he breathed after teasing her with the tip of his tongue. She heard her name catch in his throat. "I love you," he said, as if he were discovering the words all over again.

She laughed, a little breathlessly. "And I love you."

His teeth teased the pad of her thumb. "Say it," he growled. "Admit that you've changed your mind."

Suddenly, she was standing back on the balcony of the Kennedy Center. She was enchanted by moonlight, by the magnetic power of the man beside her. She was determined to stand fast, to be absolutely, positively, one hundred percent certain that she was doing what was best for her child. Not necessarily for her. Not for her body that sparked and sighed, that longed for pure, physical release.

Not yet. He loved her, and she loved him. But she had made a promise outside of their relationship, beyond the magic that bound them together. She had made a vow for their child. She would not, could not, give in to her driving need until she was well and truly married.

She sagged back against the mattress, fighting to catch her breath.

Of course, Ethan understood her decision. She heard his own ragged sigh as he released her wrist. She recognized his muffled groan as he pulled away from her, as he eased up the sheets from the foot of the bed, as he covered her with all the chaste care of a nursemaid.

But then he lay down beside her. With crisp cotton between them, he gathered her hair to her nape, smoothing it down her back. He folded an arm around her, spreading his fingers across her shielded belly. He whispered for her to relax. To trust him. To sleep.

And she did.

Chapter Eight

Five days later, Sloane sat on the flagstone patio at the back of Ethan's home, trying to convince herself that she was enjoying the book she was reading. The day was unseasonably mild, absent of D.C.'s legendary humidity. Sloane had staked out one of Ethan's chaise longues, settling in with a tall glass of decaffeinated iced tea, a poor substitute for the double espresso she craved.

Her attention wandered from her book, and she gazed out at the brilliant emerald lawn, at the black-and-white patch that was Daisy, sleeping in the shade beneath a crape myrtle tree. The puppy had insisted on a long game of fetch, repeatedly chasing after a tennis ball that Sloane had obediently thrown, over and over and over, thrilled that the animal's heart murmur wasn't inhibiting her play. For now. Finally exhausted, Daisy was snoozing, something that Sloane wished she was able to do.

She hadn't slept at all the night before, and not much for the entire week before that.

She had set her cell phone on the table beside her chair, its ringer turned to maximum volume. She had no idea whether Dr. Morton was going to phone her or Ethan, but she didn't want to risk missing the call.

The days of waiting for amnio results had crept by, stretching and contorting, drumming on her nerves until she'd thought that she would go mad. Every morning, she had stared at her new computer, telling herself that it was time to dig into the Hope Project, to finish the website. Every afternoon, she had glanced at her electronic files, tried to concentrate. Every evening, she had given up, telling herself that there was plenty of time, that she could work on Hope later.

Matters weren't helped by Ethan's near-total absence from the house. After their reconciliation on the Fourth of July, he had practically disappeared from her life. She knew that he didn't regret telling her that he loved her. He wasn't punishing her for her decision to stand by her vow. He sent messages through James, and he'd found time for a few bantering emails. It was just that he had to work late one night, and then he got called out of town to Mexico on an emergency production matter. That trip merged into a long-scheduled conference in San Francisco, another two nights of absence.

Sloane knew that Ethan had returned to Washington the night before. She'd heard him walk down the hallway after midnight, pause outside her door. She'd waited for him to turn the knob, to look in on her, to say something, anything. But he'd walked away without disturbing her. He'd been gone by the time she rose for breakfast, and she'd eaten yet another egg-white omelet, with only James for company.

Five days. Five days of loneliness, of uncertainty, of desperate, aching worry about the child inside her. Was this what her entire married life would be like?

Sighing as her tension ratcheted even tighter, she climbed to her feet and walked to the edge of the patio. To her left, she could see a patch of bright green grass, the sod that the gardeners had laid down once they'd rooted out the dead oak tree. The edges of the new grass were already starting to blur, to melt into the flawless expanse of the rest of the lawn.

She heard the door to the house open behind her, but she didn't bother to turn around. It was certain to be James, coming to ask her what she wanted for lunch. She appreciated his kindness, but she wasn't sure that she could stand another hour facing his patient smile, another meal sharing meaningless stories. Maybe she would just take Daisy for a walk, a long, meandering exploration of the neighborhood.

"Sloane."

Ethan's voice. Her name on his lips jolted through her like an electric wire. She whirled to face him as he closed the distance between them, holding out a single sheet of paper like an invitation to the prom.

She could see the energy lighting up his face, read the excitement that sparked his hazel eyes. The sunshine caught the gold in his hair, spinning back to her like confetti. Her fingers trembled, even though she knew what was written on that paper, even though she understood that it had to carry good news, given Ethan's reaction.

He watched as Sloane took the medical report from him. He saw her glance at the heading, acknowledge her name on the appropriate line, his name beneath. She barely paused when she got to the baby's gender, to the unequivocal statement that they were having a daughter.

It took her longer to parse the dense medical jargon of the next paragraph, the complicated confirmation that their little girl was healthy. No Hartwell genetic curse. No problems at all.

Sloane looked at him, her blue eyes wide, her chin tilted to a defiant angle. "Just as I said," she declared.

Even as she teased him, Sloane's exhaustion crumbled away. She felt as if she were awakening from a long, dream-torn sleep, like she was blooming in the fresh light of dawn. She laughed as Ethan closed the distance between them. His lips slanted over hers with a new urgency. It seemed as if he was kissing her for the first time, building new bonds, tying her closer than she'd ever been to any man.

A lifetime later, he finally broke away. Her knees trembled at the sensations he'd raised within her, and he gathered her close, folding her into his rock-solid arms. One confident hand spread across the back of her head, soothing, supporting. She buried her face against the white broadcloth of his shirt and breathed in the woodsy smell that was uniquely his.

She was comforted by his gesture, reassured. Ethan truly understood her need for there to be a complete emotional bond between them, something greater, something deeper than the constant thrum of physical excitement that beat inside her anytime he was near.

He laughed as he gathered her close. Certainly it had not been his first instinct to break off that kiss. He longed to let his hands roam, to ease beneath her green blouse, to tweak the pebbled nipples that he knew stood out against her bra. But fair was fair. He had promised.

And that promise had led to a miracle. A healthy baby girl. *His* healthy baby girl.

For the first time since he had learned that Sloane was

pregnant, Ethan actually let himself enjoy the thought. He allowed himself to picture a future, a life shared for decades. He finally let himself think beyond the mock marriage he'd stumbled into, the pretend commitment that he'd told himself he could walk away from if his worst fears had been confirmed. This was Sloane he was thinking about, the woman that he loved. The woman who, impossibly, had said that she loved him back. He couldn't leave her. Not now. Not ever.

He only had one more hurdle: meeting Grandmother's January deadline. Now that he and Sloane were united in their happiness, there should be no problem defeating that absurd ultimatum. He wasn't a fool, though. He wasn't going to tell Sloane about Grandmother's ridiculous requirement. There was no reason to disturb her with facts that had absolutely no shred of meaning.

Instead, he murmured against her hair, "That just leaves one small thing."

"Hmm?" Sloane murmured, unwilling to break the perfect moment, to topple the steady, comforting balance that had settled over them.

"We need to set a date for the wedding. I've been thinking about September sixth."

She started to laugh, thinking that he must be joking. When she pulled away enough to see his face, though, she knew that he was completely serious. "September sixth? Why?"

"It's the Sunday of Labor Day weekend. Our guests will have time to travel here, time to return home on Monday."

"But it's less than two months away!" She caught his hand and guided him back to the chaise longue. They sat at the same time, as if they were beginning a formal business negotiation.

He shrugged at her protest. "We can get everything done between now and then. I was thinking that we'd get married here at the house. That limits access for the press, and we don't have to worry about securing a facility on relatively short notice. It won't be a problem to line up caterers, of course. That's just a financial transaction."

Just a financial transaction. Sloane settled a hand over her waist. Over her *daughter*. "I'll be as big as a house by September!" She'd never considered herself a vain woman, never thought that she would care about appearances like that. But she was only getting married once in her life. Only building a family once in her life. A part of her wanted everything about that experience to be absolutely perfect. "I assumed that we'd wait until after the baby is here. Get through the first few months of chaos with a newborn, and then get married in June."

His eyes darkened, as if she'd suggested something impossible. For just a moment, she saw him consider some argument, contemplate words that he discarded with a tense shrug, with a quick bite of his lip. Instead, he settled his fingers over hers, rippling a fresh wave of energy through her. "I don't care if you're the size of the Taj Mahal. Sloane, I made a promise to you, back at the Kennedy Center, and you know that I'll keep it. But I'm not going to lie to you. I want you. Now, here, on this patio, on the grass, in my bed." He cupped her face with his free hand, snagging her gaze with an intensity that rocked her to her core. "Don't make me wait until next summer. Don't do that to me, love. To us."

Her skin was on fire where he touched her; every nerve ending sparked with energy. She was catapulted back to their night at the Eastern, the night that had created their daughter. Everything had been simple then.

She had listened to her body, trusted its desires. Trusted Ethan.

He shifted the hand that spread across her belly, raising his fingers to her neck. Seemingly without effort, he found pressure points above her nape, tiny anchors of tension. He kneaded away stress that she hadn't realized she was carrying, caressing her with all the care he had shown her as a lover. She closed her eyes and let her head fall back, let her body luxuriate in the attention.

Floating on a sea of warmth, she knew that she wanted more. She wanted to feel his skin against every inch of her, wanted to press herself against his broad chest, twine her legs between his. She was melting beside him, longing transforming her into a mindless puddle.

September. She pulled her thoughts together enough to focus on September. She could wait until then. Just.

She settled her ready mouth on his, shuddering at the unexpected sensation as his teeth closed on her lower lip for a single, fleeting moment. She barely managed to pull away from the reeling kiss. Somehow, though, she found the wherewithal to say, "You drive a hard bargain, Mr. Hartwell."

His rough laugh against her throat nearly made her demand an overnight elopement. "You'll do it, then? We can marry in September?"

"September," she said, the three syllables getting lost in a sigh of pleasure. Ethan folded his arms around her, leaning her back against the chaise longue, cushioning her body as his embrace became even more enthusiastic.

Sloane nearly lost herself in the waves of sensation washing over her body. Before she could summon the will to pull away, though, before she could restore them both to the promise they had made, she was startled by a chorus of hysterical yapping.

Daisy.

The puppy had awakened from her nap. Seeing Ethan, she had galloped toward the patio. Now, she was bouncing up and down as if her legs were spring-loaded. She acted as if she hadn't seen her beloved master for years.

Ethan collapsed his head against Sloane's shoulder. "Quite a little chaperone you have there, Ms. Davenport."

Sloane laughed a bit unsteadily. "She has our best interest at heart."

Heart. The word should have made them both cringe, should have reminded them of the illness that would eventually steal Daisy away from them. That future, though, was far away on this sunny July afternoon, on the day when they had discovered that their daughter was going to be healthy, was going to be born with a complete life ahead of her. No cloud could spoil the joy of the letter that Ethan had delivered from the doctor's office.

"Sit," Sloane said to Daisy, adding a hand signal to emphasize the command. The puppy was too excited, though, to mind. "Sit!" Sloane repeated.

Ethan smiled indulgently as the silly little dog kept up her barking. He pushed himself off Sloane carefully, taking care not to harm her in any way. When he turned to the bouncing Daisy, he pushed authority into his voice, "Sit, Daisy," he commanded. The dog dropped to her haunches as if she'd been trained in the circus.

Sloane laughed. "Well, I guess we know who she thinks is the pushover, don't we? There's no reason for her to listen to me."

Ethan ruffled the puppy's ears, telling her that she was a good dog. The words came to him automatically, easily, but his mind was already drifting elsewhere. Sloane had agreed to the September date. He would meet Grandmother's deadline, with months to spare. He couldn't imagine being a happier man.

The following Monday, Hartwell Genetics released a formal engagement announcement, officially confirming all the gossip of the past several weeks, declaring to the entire world that Sloane and Ethan were getting married on September sixth. Sloane still felt they were rushing things, but she understood, and even appreciated, Ethan's reasons for moving forward. He certainly reinforced their decision often enough—cornering her in the kitchen with a few well-placed kisses, passing her in the hallway with a knowing caress that turned her knees to jelly, and often, oh, so often, repeating the words that made her heart soar: I love you.

By noon on Monday, Hartwell Genetics's marketing department had already secured the finest caterer in town, booked a band and arranged for a photographer. Ethan's wealth made so many things easy.

It also, though, made things complicated. By midafternoon, the phone calls started at the house. These were contacts from the legitimate press—the business papers and magazines that would never have stooped to report the earlier gossip. James handled them all, answering with a reserved "No comment," politely but firmly refusing to provide any additional information about where Mr. Hartwell had met Ms. Davenport, about where Ms. Davenport was currently residing, about rumors that a baby might be on the way, rushing the date of the nuptials.

Retreating from the jangle of phones, Sloane closed the door to the library. It was comforting there in the dark, wood-paneled room, surrounded by books and the heft of heavy leather furniture. She curled up on the dark green couch with her laptop, grateful for the chance finally to dig back into the Hope Project.

She made the mistake of checking her favorite news site before she began her work. Her engagement was splashed all over the page. It turned out that a lot of people had an interest in Ethan Hartwell and his matrimonial plans. The financial pages all discussed the likely impact on Hartwell Genetics. The health care reporters speculated on whether any new products would be brought to market in the fourth quarter. The gossip pages continued to report their usual mash of confused half-truths, focusing on Sloane's mysterious background. She didn't know whether to be pleased or annoyed that she was painted as a conniving fortune hunter by one publication, an innocent victim of Ethan's playboy ways by another and a business partner in disguise by yet a third.

As she shook her head in disbelief, her cell phone rang. She glanced at the Caller ID. Ethan.

"Surviving the storm?" he asked. She could hear the smile in his voice, picture the curve of his lips as he formed the question. Immediately, she pictured those lips put to better use, and she had to shake her head, to return her concentration to the matter at hand.

"I had no idea that so many people would care about what we do with our personal lives!"

"Just imagine what would happen if they knew the *truly* personal details I could share with them." His growl ignited a blush that tingled from the roots of her hair to her toes. "Where are you now?" he asked.

"In the library." She made her voice as prim and proper as she could. If she gave in to the invitation barely hidden behind his words she would never get any work done that afternoon.

"What are you wearing?" he whispered.

"A white blouse buttoned up to my neck, a black skirt with a bustle that hangs to my ankles and tiny boots that pinch my feet," she said, smoothing her hand over her T-shirt and shorts.

"Are the boots made out of leather?"

She couldn't help but laugh at the hopeful note in his voice. "How's work?" she asked. "Are you able to get anything done, with everyone digging for more information? James has been fielding calls here nonstop."

"I've issued my 'no comments.' I've also accepted a half-dozen invitations."

"Invitations?"

"Drinks here. Dinners there. I'm only saying yes to the ones I absolutely can't afford for us to skip. Do you hate me?"

She laughed at the worried note in his voice. "How could I hate you? Just make sure I end up with all the dates in my calendar."

"The most important one is in a month. Grandmother is throwing a cocktail party in our honor. At her apartment, downtown."

"Her apartment? Fine. I assume there will only be a handful of guests?"

"You haven't seen Grandmother's apartment. She has the entire top floor of the Waverly."

Sloane's enthusiasm flagged, but she knew that they'd both be happier if she kept a positive attitude. "A cocktail party for a hundred of our closest friends. Sounds grand. It'll cost you, though. I'll need something appropriate to wear."

His chortle thrilled her over the phone line. "Whatever you desire. Speaking of which, let's get back to those leather boots...."

Ethan drank deeply from his beer, grateful that he and Zach were viewing the Nationals baseball game from the air-conditioned comfort of the luxury box owned by Zach's law firm. "You owe me, buddy," he said. "Owe me big time."

"Wait a minute," Zach said, gesturing around the well-appointed room. "I thought *you* were supposed to be grateful to *me,* for bringing you to the game."

"I consider this a small down payment on the real debt, my friend." Ethan paused to watch the visiting pitcher step up to the plate. Three pitches, and the Nationals had nailed the third out of the inning. Music started to play as the team ran in from the field.

Zach sighed in mock apology. "And what have I done this time?"

"Made a small fortune for the Good to the Bone dog obedience school." Ethan pretended to glare as Zach laughed. "I've had one of their instructors on call for a week. Whenever Sloane heads out on an errand, James squeezes in a quick session with Daisy. So far, she's mastered sit, stay and down. I just hope that she gets the hang of 'heel' pretty soon. That one's harder to practice, without Sloane figuring out what we're working on."

"I never thought I'd see the day when Ethan Hartwell was worried about training a puppy."

"Yeah, well, there are a lot of things I never thought I'd be doing." Ethan stared out at the baseball diamond, losing track of the pitch sequence as he thought about the night before. He had taken to walking Sloane to her bedroom each night. He stood on the threshold of the guest suite like a high school kid hanging out on a front porch, worried that his girlfriend's father was standing just inside the front door.

Like that overeager teen, he had leaned in to kiss Sloane good-night. Before he was fully aware of what he was doing, he had eased his hands beneath the loose T-shirt that she wore. The garment was casual, but her hidden bra was not. He had caught his breath as his palms passed over a line of lace that left little to his over-heated imagination. Immediately, he could picture her breasts straining to be free. Trying to ignore the arrow that tugged at his groin, he had eased his fingers beneath the fabric edge, gliding around to Sloane's back, to the delicate clasp that kept her covered, kept her safe. She had sighed as he flicked the fastener open, her delicate breath immediately reminding him of the way she had lain beneath him at the Eastern.

Another minute, and it would have been too late. Another minute, and they both would have cast away their silly vow of chastity. He'd recognized the power-ful need on her face, the desire that had welled up in her eyes like an entire conversation.

And then Daisy had come bounding up the stairs, eager for her last walk of the night and her usual dog biscuit treat. Ethan had managed not to swear as he bent down to ruffle the excited puppy's ears. Sloane had ac-tually laughed, closing her door before either of them could walk down a tantalizing—and thoroughly physi-cally satisfying—road of regrets.

Now, Zach whistled, long and low. "You are a total goner, aren't you? And here I thought you were never going to give up your title to Bachelor of the Year."

Ethan shook his head, forcing his thoughts back to the stadium, back to the good-natured ribbing of his best friend. "Believe me, I never thought I'd do it, either."

"Then it's not just because of Margaret? Not because of the stock transfer?" The two men rarely talked about Margaret Hartwell. Zach took attorney-client confidentiality seriously. In this case, though, they were both fully aware of the transfer provisions that would benefit AFAA if Ethan failed to conform.

Ethan's lips curled into a sardonic grin. "It started that way. I figured I could kill two birds with one stone—keep Grandmother's stock in the family, and push every single one of her controlling, manipulative, marriage-minded buttons—all by choosing a woman she never expected me to marry."

"But now?"

"Now, I just want Sloane. If Grandmother disapproved and said that she was still going to donate her stock, I wouldn't care. I'd still marry Sloane. Tomorrow, if we could."

"Man," Zach said, shaking his head and popping open two more beers. "You really have it bad." Ethan heard a faint touch of jealousy in the other man's voice. He laughed, and they turned back to the ball game, just as the Nationals' cleanup hitter knocked a home run out of the park.

Sloane picked up her purse and hurried back into the library. "Jeanine," she said. "Thank you for being so patient!"

The skinny redhead glanced up from Daisy, who was sitting quietly in the middle of the thick Turkish rug, eyes focused intently on the trainer's right hand. "No problem!"

"Should I make out that check to you, or to Doggie-B-Good?"

"The company name is fine," Jeanine said. Then she turned back to Daisy and snapped her fingers. "Good Daisy," she said, releasing the pet from the "sit" command. Daisy started to wag her entire hind quarters in excitement at the praise.

Sloane laughed. "I cannot believe how she's caught on to all of the commands!"

"Some dogs just learn really quickly," Jeanine said. "They all *want* to be good. That makes everything work out in their pack. Isn't that right, Daisy? Don't you want to be a good puppy?"

For answer, Daisy yapped once. Sloane handed over the check. "I really appreciate your coming over here at such crazy times. It's just that I want this training to be a surprise, for Ethan. It would be easy enough if I just had to wait for him to be out of town, but I don't want James to know, either. He'd spill the beans, for sure."

"I completely understand. You'll call me when you're ready to schedule our next lesson?"

"Absolutely," Sloane promised. She walked the dog trainer to the front door, then settled back on the couch.

As she adjusted her laptop computer across her legs, Daisy whined from the floor. "Down!" Sloane commanded. The little dog dropped to the floor like a pro. "Good dog," Sloane said. She would have loved to have the puppy on the couch beside her, but she knew that would only create problems when the Old English sheepdog reached her full growth. A little discipline was good for a dog.

Discipline was good for computer programmers, too. Sloane had spent the past week trying to work out yet another problem with the Hope Project website. She knew the drawing module that she wanted to link to the front page. The software worked exactly as she intended when she used it in isolation. But every single time that she plugged it into one of the diagnostic packages, it locked up the entire website.

"Okay, Daisy," Sloane muttered under her breath. "I am *going* to figure this out. I'm not going to bed until this section works."

Two hours later, Sloane regretted her rash promise. Her eyes felt sandy. She was thirsty. Her back twinged from sitting too long in the same position. She was about to give up on the entire evening, declare the night a loss, when she heard Ethan's key in the front door.

Daisy leaped up and skittered into the hallway, yipping a greeting. "I'm in here!" Sloane called out, when she could make herself heard over the din. She set her computer on the floor and swung herself into a sitting position.

Ethan came into the room, Daisy at his heels. "Sit!" he said to the excited dog, and Sloane was secretly proud to see how quickly Daisy responded. Sloane couldn't wait to show Ethan all of Daisy's tricks, to put the little dog through her paces. Soon enough… All they needed to master was the command to heel.

Ethan sank onto the couch beside Sloane. "You're not still working, are you?"

She smiled ruefully. "I have gone over every single line of this program a hundred times. I *cannot* figure out why it won't launch properly."

He made a comforting noise and shifted beside her. When his strong hands fell on her shoulders, she melted against him. He started to knead her taut muscles, backing up his gentle touch with just enough strength to force out the knots she'd acquired in a long evening of frustration. "Why don't you tell me what you're trying to do? Sometimes talking about something makes it all come clear."

She shifted a little, giving him access to her shoulder blades, to the middle of her back. His questing fingers obliged, and she let the rhythm that he established guide her thoughts. "Everyone who wants to use the drawing module has to register when they come onto the website. It's a security step, to keep individual children anonymous within the system, and to let users save their work between sessions."

He made a wordless sound of understanding, walking his fingers down another few vertebrae. She hadn't realized how tight her spine had become. She let her head fall forward, stretching out the muscles in her neck, and then she continued. "The registration sets correctly whenever users immediately go into the drawing package. But if they stop first at one of the information pages, then they're locked out of the entire system."

She started to tighten her hands into fists, falling back into her frustration, but Ethan's gentle touch reminded her to exhale, to let her body relax. It was as if his hands had the power to wash all of her thoughts out of her mind. He could clear her memory with nothing more than the tips of his fingers and the smooth, steady sound of his breath.

Clear her memory.

The art program cleared its memory every time it was called up, giving each user a clean slate for creating pictures. That was a feature, an easy way to let children start each session fresh, without being dragged down into whatever drawings they had made before, whatever problems they had been working on in the past.

"That's it!" she said. "I just have to tell it explicitly

to remember the password! It should forget everything else but remember that information!"

Energized by her breakthrough, she pulled away from Ethan, snatching up her computer from the floor and typing away on the program.

Ethan watched her single-minded enthusiasm as she worked. He loved the way that she focused on the monitor, the way her eyes narrowed just a fraction as she worked through each line of text. Most people would have walked away from the Hope Project by now. Most people would have given up, written off the idea as a good one, but too complex, too difficult to make real.

But not Sloane. She was willing to fight for what she believed in. She was willing to do whatever had to be done.

And Ethan had to admit that he found that drive, that devotion, more compelling than anything else about the woman he was going to marry. Sure, he enjoyed showing her fine things, introducing her to the ballet, to the best restaurants in Washington. Absolutely, he reveled in her body, as much as she was willing to share. But her mind was what truly captivated him—her absolute dedication to her beliefs of right and wrong, and her certainty that she could change the world for the better.

With a flourish, she pressed a key, hunching forward as she waited to see if the program would finally work. Ethan caught his breath as she did, waiting, hoping. When a bright rainbow spilled across the screen, Sloane shouted her laughter. "That's it!" she cried. "You solved it!"

He caught her close as she flung her arms around him, embracing him with the enthusiasm of a high school cheerleader. "I didn't have anything to do with it," he protested until she stopped him with a kiss. "But if that's the way you want to thank me," he continued when he'd surfaced from her energetic attention, "I'm happy to pretend."

"Pretend!" She pulled him close in another overwhelming hug. "That's what I love about being with you. Neither one of us has to pretend a thing!"

She pulled away so that she could show him how the art package functioned, how a child could use it to work through worries and fears. Ethan listened to every word. He had to. He was trying to drown out the little voice that clamored at the back of his head, nagging him to tell Sloane about his grandmother's ultimatum. He should stop pretending, once and for all.

And he would. Very, very soon, he promised himself. For now, he concentrated on the Hope Project, and everything that Sloane was going to accomplish.

Chapter Nine

The next two weeks flew by. Ethan had three business trips—to San Francisco, to Paris, to Montreal.

Sloane missed him while he was gone, but every reunion was sweeter than the last. Each time, he entered the house like a returning hero, finding her on the patio, in the bedroom, staking claim to her with kisses that threatened to steal her breath away forever.

Coming back from Canada, he found her working in the library, her legs stretched out on the green leather couch, her laptop balanced across her thighs. Daisy greeted him with enthusiasm, wriggling with excitement, as if he'd been gone for years rather than forty-eight hours. Nevertheless, the puppy complied with his command to sit; she behaved like a true show dog.

Sloane started to stand up when he came in, but he quickly settled beside her. He took her bare feet onto his lap, finding the tender point at each arch, smoothing away tension with the unerring weight of his thumb.

"Mmm," she said, scrunching lower on the couch so that her head rested against the padded arm. "Do I know you?"

"How quickly they forget," he growled in mock disdain. His fingers tickled up her bare legs, tracing the hem of her shorts against her thighs. "Or maybe you have an endless line of men, waiting to rub your feet?"

For answer, she shut the computer, making sure that the lid snicked closed before she set it on the luxurious Turkish carpet. She would hate to lose hours of hard work. The Hope Project was nearly done; she'd be ready to have beta testers work through the website in another week or two.

Her hands free, she knelt on the couch, enjoying the flare of pleased surprise in Ethan's eyes as he realized that the top two buttons of her blouse were open. His hands settled on her waist, steadying her, pulling her closer.

The action triggered a flutter deep inside of her. "Oh!"

"What?" he asked, only the tightening of his fingers over her hipbones betraying anxiety.

"The baby! I felt her move!"

The look of joy that spread across Ethan's face filled her heart even more than the sudden realization that her baby—their daughter—was growing, was ever closer to joining them. Another flutter rippled through her insides.

"Is this the first time you've felt her?" Ethan asked. He kept his voice low, even though he knew the baby couldn't hear them, even though he knew that he could not possibly disturb their daughter.

"I thought I felt her move, maybe a week ago. And again, the morning that you left for Montreal." Sloane's smile was wide, her blue eyes bright with laughter. "This is the first time I've been certain, though."

Reaching underneath Sloane's blouse, he settled his palm across her belly. He felt a sudden tremble ripple across her skin, but he knew *that* motion was caused by him, summoned by his touch. He waited, holding his breath.

"There!" Sloane said.

He shook his head, trying not to feel cheated, not to feel left out. "Nothing," he said. "Not yet." Still, seeing the excitement that flushed Sloane's cheeks, he found himself laughing. "Soon enough, though. Give our little ballerina another couple of months, and you'll be begging her to sit still for a while."

"Never!" Sloane's laughter filled his chest with a fierce protectiveness, and he gathered her close to his side, kissing the top of her head, all the while maintaining contact with their baby.

"I hope she doesn't bother you too much at dinner tonight."

Sloane shook her head. Of course the baby wouldn't be a bother. Then, she remembered. "That's right! We're meeting those board members, for dinner downtown!" She looked at her watch. "Another engagement party. That's why you're home early."

The smile that he turned on her was as lazy as a summer afternoon. "That, and I wanted to see you."

He was rewarded with a deep kiss. A deep kiss, and her hands roaming over his back, and then the confession, "I missed you."

"All of this travel has been ridiculous. It'll slow down for the rest of the month. Washington practically goes to sleep in August. We used to travel, Grandmother and I, to a different country every year."

"I can't imagine what that would be like!" She sighed, thinking that their daughter would get to enjoy that sort of life, would thrive on exciting experiences.

She shivered as Ethan's inquisitive fingers did something thoroughly unapproved with the waistband of her shorts. She caught his hand in hers, needing to protect herself from his distraction. "Which was your favorite trip?" she asked, as if his childhood travels were the most fascinating thing in the universe.

He laughed, but he played along, knowing full well what she was doing. "Paris, probably. Grandmother and I spent an entire day in the Musée d'Orsay, looking at the Impressionist paintings."

"I had no idea you were such an art lover."

"I wasn't," he admitted. "But the tour guide Grandmother hired was a totally stunning French girl, with the sexiest accent…"

Sloane hurled a throw pillow at him.

"What?" he protested. "I was fourteen years old, and very impressionable."

"I can only imagine," she said dryly.

"What about you? What was your favorite summer?"

She paused before she answered, really thought about the question. Summers were always a challenge when she was young; the long days seemed to add a special strain to life in a foster family. But when she was a teenager, she had volunteered at the Art Institute of Chicago. "The year I turned sixteen," she said. "I spent every day down at the art museum. I developed a series of tours for little kids, five-minute lectures that taught them the basics of art history. I just loved seeing the connections those kids made, the way they figured things out."

"And the Hope Project grew from there," he said.

"With a few thousand steps in between."

"I guess it really is the things that spark for us when we're young," he said. "My grandfather and I used to play Monopoly. He was absolutely cutthroat at the game, wouldn't give an inch, even when I was just starting to learn the rules. But I ended up loving everything about it—the deals we'd make to swap properties, the strategy of building hotels on some squares and not on others."

"You don't talk about your family very much. I've never even heard you mention your grandfather."

"He died ten years ago. I was only twenty-three. Sometimes I wonder what he'd think about me. About the person I've become."

Sloane heard the yearning in Ethan's voice, the desire to be accepted. To be loved. "I think he'd be very proud," she said.

Ethan cleared his throat and pushed himself to his feet. The movement caused Daisy to dance backward and forward. "We should get ready, if we're going to get to the restaurant on time. I'll walk this fierce beast before we go."

They made it to the restaurant with ten minutes to spare, and they had a charming evening with the board members. As they did three nights later, when they got together with Ethan's med school roommates and their wives. And Ethan's business school friends a few nights after that.

Sloane was consistently astonished that Ethan knew so many people. He shrugged it off, as easily as he shrugged off his enormous fortune, the tremendous success of Hartwell Genetics. He'd lived lots of lives, he said, first as Margaret's grandson, then as a doctor, then as a successful entrepreneur. There were a lot of social circles to intersect.

A lot of dinner parties to attend.

Sloane needed to put Ethan's credit card back in circulation. At five months and counting, she was truly beginning to show. She felt marvelous, full of energy, as if she were only now coming fully awake after those first few months of nausea and discomfort. She suspected that, down the road, she'd be awkward and uncomfortable, but for now, she was thrilled by the ease of her pregnancy, by the simple presence of her ever-growing daughter.

Her increased energy let her finally finish the Hope Project. In fact, she was just saving the final computer file, when her cell phone rang. She glanced at the unfamiliar number, surprised that anyone was tracking her down that way. Suspecting that Ethan might be trying to reach her from an unknown line, she answered. "Hello?"

"Ms. Davenport?"

"Yes. Who is this please?"

"My name is Lionel Hampton. I'm afraid we haven't met before, but Margaret Hartwell suggested that I give you a call."

Sloane's heart leaped into her throat. Lionel Hampton. The executive director of the American Foundation for the Advancement of the Arts. Her ex-boss's boss's boss. "Mr. Hampton," she said, hoping that she hadn't let too many seconds tick away as she battled her surprise.

"Is this a good time for us to talk?"

Sloane glanced at her computer screen, at the culmination of five years of work, all wrapped up in the Hope Project. "Yes," she said, and then she realized that she'd made her statement sound like a question. She cleared her throat. "How can I help you, Mr. Hampton?"

"I had lunch with my dear friend Margaret this afternoon. She informed me that you and Ethan Hartwell are to be married next month. Please accept my very best wishes."

"Of course," Sloane said, feeling her forehead crease as she frowned. What had Margaret done?

"I don't have to tell you that Margaret is one of your biggest fans." Sloane wasn't about to say otherwise, even if the news was something of a surprise. Mr. Hampton went on, as if Sloane had agreed wholeheartedly. "I was just telling Margaret that we are trying to expand our mission here at AFAA, that we want to have more of an impact on the world beyond the traditional four corners of cultural stewardship. As soon as Margaret mentioned your art therapy project for at-risk foster children, I knew that we had a perfect match."

"A perfect match?" Sloane wondered if her mind was playing tricks on her, if she was hearing things.

Mr. Hampton cleared his throat. "With Margaret's generous assistance, AFAA is about to create a new center, a division that will specialize in advancing the arts curriculum for children. Margaret speaks very, very highly of you, Ms. Davenport. I would love to offer you a position as the director of our new program."

Just like that. Margaret wrote a check, pulled some strings and Sloane landed the job of her dreams. Months of résumés, frantic nights wondering whether she would ever find another job, all erased by her wealthy future grandmother-in-law's largesse.

Even if Sloane could accept such a gift, there was one substantial problem. "Mr. Hampton, are you aware of the fact that I worked for AFAA? That I was dismissed from my position back in March?"

"Oh, yes. That." A prim sound rattled over the line, a cross between a cleared throat and a cough. "I understand that there was some confusion about our Spring Auction, and that one of our managers may have acted a little precipitously...."

Sloane shook her head. She couldn't believe what she was hearing. "I was fired out of hand, for something that had nothing to do with my performance."

"And I wish that I'd been made aware of the circumstances at the time. Ms. Davenport, I do hope that you can set aside any negative feelings that you might have about our organization. To that end, I'd love to meet you for lunch, say next Monday? We could discuss this matter further, along with the possibilities of our exciting new center. I do hope that you'll say yes."

Sloane considered her options. She could refuse to meet with the man. She could send him back to Margaret in defeat, mostly likely returning a large check.

Or she could meet with him. She could talk to him about his new center. She could explain, in her own words, just what her project was about and what she knew she could accomplish.

Sure, they might not be able to get past her prior experience at AFAA. But she'd be a fool not to try. Wouldn't she?

"Thank you, Mr. Hampton. I'd love to discuss this matter further."

She heard the gratitude in his voice as he specified a restaurant, as he thanked her for agreeing to consider the possibility, as he offered her his very best wishes for a wonderful weekend. Sloane stared at the phone for a long time after she hung up from the call.

So. This must be what it was like, to have the power and prestige of the Hartwell name behind her. This was what she could anticipate for the rest of her life, as Ethan's wife. This was the way that doors would open for their daughter.

As if in response, the baby chose that moment to kick against her insides. Sloane smiled. She couldn't imagine what her meeting with Mr. Hampton would be like. She could hardly give him the details about why she'd been dismissed from AFAA. Of course, if the man had done his homework, then it wouldn't be necessary to give him any information at all. And if Margaret's check had already cleared the bank, the entire matter would be moot. The only thing that Sloane needed to do was thank her future grandmother-in-law.

Three days later, she had the opportunity, at the engagement party Margaret was hosting for Ethan and Sloane.

Sloane took greater care than usual dressing for the party, feeling like a debutante, poised on the edge of her formal introduction to polite society. Sitting beside Ethan in the back of the Town Car, she stared out the window as the streets of D.C. rushed by. She ran over names and faces in her mind, hoping that she didn't stumble over any important introductions.

Ethan laughed when she asked him to fill her in, one more time, on the names of the Hartwell Genetics board members. "Relax. It's a cocktail party. We'll have a couple of drinks, and then we'll leave."

"Easy for you to say." She sighed. "You actually get to drink something with alcohol. Just one glass of wine... that would make this so much easier."

"What if you had something to look forward to?"

His arch tone was enough to bring a blush to her cheeks. Good. The color brought out the sparkle in her eyes. "Like what?" she asked, faking a tone of perfect innocence. She knew exactly what she was doing to him. She laughed as he shifted beside her, adjusting his suddenly uncomfortable summer-weight trousers.

God, she was beautiful tonight. The forest-green of her dress set off her eyes, complemented the jet-black hair that she wore down, perfectly straight, a challenge to all those women who thought that primping and preening would make them more attractive. Her body was responding to the baby's needs; every curve that had initially sparked his attention was more voluptuous than ever.

He considered ordering the driver to take a detour. After all, what would his grandmother do if they were late? She couldn't very well interrogate him in public, could she?

Ethan shook his head. Grandmother could do exactly that. And she would, too.

No. Better to go to the party. Hear a few short speeches in honor of himself and the woman who was the mother of his child. Eat some incredibly overpriced appetizers. Drink some of the world's finest alcohol. And then come home, to see what he could do about raising another smile on Sloane's lips.

Ethan's obvious appreciation of her appearance made Sloane a little less apprehensive as the car pulled into the sweeping circular driveway of the Waverly condominium. A doorman helped her out of the backseat as Ethan gave brisk instructions to the driver.

As they stood in the elevator, Ethan took her hand, twining his fingers with hers. He squeezed once, meeting her eyes in the mirrored door, and she smiled back at him, cursing herself for feeling nervous about a simple party.

Every building in Washington was subject to a height restriction. There were only twelve stories to travel in the privacy of the elevator car. All too soon, the door opened. All too soon, they were ushered into a stunning apartment. All too soon, Sloane was swept up in the chaos of a party in full swing.

It seemed as if a dozen men waited to shake Ethan's hand, to offer him their hearty congratulations. She pasted a smile on her lips as he was pulled away from her. Before she could begin the hard work of finding someone to chat with, Margaret glided across the room.

The older woman wore a dramatic pink suit with wide lapels and a cinched waist. Sloane couldn't imagine anyone else wearing the outfit. She also couldn't imagine anyone questioning Margaret's choice—not with the triple strand of pearls that hung halfway down her chest, an authoritative reminder of Margaret's wealth.

Sloane was surprised that Margaret folded her into an embrace. She could smell baby powder on the older woman, along with just a hint of lilac. Margaret spoke first. "You look lovely this evening, dear."

"Thank you," Sloane said, a little surprised by the warmth of the greeting. "It's so kind of you to throw a party in our honor."

"You're feeling well?" Margaret glanced at Sloane's waist, her smile indulgent.

"Very well, thank you."

Margaret switched her attention to Sloane's face. The older woman's gaze was intense, as if she were suddenly communicating in some secret language. "I want you to know how much I appreciate what you've done for Ethan. He's a changed man since he met you."

"Oh, I don't think—"

"I do," Margaret said firmly. "I can see it in his face. In the way he walks down the hallway at work. He's more relaxed, more *confident* than I've ever seen him before."

Sloane could hardly imagine Ethan being anything other than confident. Nevertheless, grandmothers viewed their grandsons through different lenses than did the rest of the world. And Sloane certainly wasn't going to argue with her hostess.

"Oh, bother," Margaret said. "The senator is waving me over. I really should be a proper hostess."

"Please," Sloane said. "Don't let me keep you." She watched, a little awestruck, as Margaret floated across the room to shake hands with one of the most influential men in Washington.

Only then did Sloane remember that she hadn't mentioned Lionel Hampton, hadn't thanked Margaret for her donation to AFAA. She gritted her teeth in exasperation. Well, there'd be another opportunity at some point in the evening.

Sloane looked around the room. This was a different world, far removed from the foster homes and uncertainty she'd known as a child. How could anyone growing up in this *not* be confident? Sloane saw Ethan standing near the grand piano, surrounded by a circle of dark-suited men. She recognized the junior senator from New York, and a Supreme Court justice, both offering their hearty congratulations.

"So much power, all in one living room."

Sloane started at the voice. She turned around to see Zach, a friendly smile brightening the lawyer's face. He held a highball glass, filled with some amber liquid and ice. His suit looked a little rumpled, and there was a spot on his tie. Sloane caught herself liking the easy-going man more than ever. She said, "Do you ever feel like you're caught up in a masquerade, and any minute now someone is going to rip off your mask?"

"Every day," Zach said, taking a sip from the glass in his hand. "Every single day."

"But you've been coming to this sort of thing for years! Don't you get used to it?"

Zach shrugged. "In a way. Ethan used to invite me when we were kids. Margaret always let him have one friend along, so that he wouldn't get *too* lonely among all the grown-ups."

"From what I hear, Margaret was probably hoping that your good behavior would rub off on him."

"It didn't work out that way. I just learned bigger and better ways to get into trouble."

Sloane answered dryly, "I can see how that would happen."

Zach laughed at her tone. "You can see why Margaret worked so hard to get Ethan to settle down. She just wanted to host one single cocktail party where he didn't cause a scandal. After all those years, I could hardly believe it, when she finally found the magic key."

"Magic key?"

Zach drank again. "You know, the whole ultimatum thing." He curled his fingers into quotation marks, as if he were reciting something Margaret had said. "A wedding by her birthday, or she was stepping down from the Board and giving everything to AFAA. I never thought it would work, but she proved me wrong. It made all those weeks of writing the stock transfer agreement worth it."

Margaret's birthday.

Everything to AFAA.

No wonder Ethan had pushed for a wedding before the baby was born.

Sloane felt the blood rush from her face. She made some halfhearted excuse to Zach, something that might actually have sounded like a joke, and then she stumbled off to the edge of the room. She needed to sit down. Needed to catch her breath. Needed to make sense out of the nightmare words Zach had just cast off so blithely.

Before Sloane could escape, though, Margaret was at the front of the room, summoning her guests to silence. Ethan broke away from his coterie of friends, crossing to Sloane with an easy smile. His fingers were light on her elbow as he said, "Time to sing for our supper."

Ethan was astonished at how pale Sloane had become. Maybe he'd been wrong to bring her here, wrong to let Grandmother plan this ridiculous party. It was so tiring to be on display, to meet and greet business acquaintances and friends. He should have put his foot down. He should have insisted that they forget about the party, about letting Margaret show them off to everyone.

Too late now.

He settled one hand across the small of Sloane's back. She shied away from him, though, as if she were burned by his touch. As if she resented his dragging her here. He scowled toward his grandmother, annoyed to see that she had finally succeeded in breaking through the cocktail party chatter. All eyes were on Margaret Hartwell.

And her eyes were on him. On him and Sloane. He leaned close and whispered, "Are you all right?"

For answer, Sloane merely pulled her arm away from him. She followed him to the front of the room, though, and he had to be content with standing next to her, fighting the urge to give her his arm to lean on, to make their excuses and get them out of the damned room altogether.

Apparently unaware of Sloane's distress, his grandmother said, "Friends! I thank you all for joining me this evening, to celebrate an event I never thought I'd live to see."

Ethan heard the good-natured laughter of the guests, heightened by the drinks they'd already enjoyed. His grandmother went on, spinning out a story about how Ethan had been a wild little boy, how he had always refused to mind her, how he had run away and hidden from her in the National Museum of Natural History. She made people laugh, recounting Ethan's first experience in the Hartwell Genetics boardroom, when he had refused to give in to a strident board member, matching age and money with his own unique brand of stubbornness.

Grandmother's voice grew suspiciously thick, though, as she lifted her glass in the air. "I see that my grandson was only conditioning me to accept his headstrong ways, preparing me to rejoice in the finest decision of his adult life. My darling Ethan has chosen to bring Sloane Davenport into our family. Ethan, Sloane, may you have many joyful years together!"

"Hear, hear!" cried the guests, and Ethan inclined his head as dozens of glasses were raised in his—in *their*—honor.

Knowing what was expected of him, he leaned down to kiss his grandmother's cheek, murmuring, "Thank you."

Her eyes sparkled as she settled a dry hand along his jaw. Her lips trembled with a surprising show of emotion. He had to admit, though, that she looked happier than she had in years. Happier, and healthier—as if she could live another eighty years.

Ethan smiled at the crowd as he slipped his arm around Sloane's waist. She felt stiff as a board next to him. Poor thing. She hadn't been in this spotlight before, hadn't been the center of attention for dozens of well-wishers. He wished that he could say something private to her, that he could whisk her away. Just a few more moments, though, a few more polite words. Then they would be done with the formal part of the evening. He'd be able to get them out of the room in half an hour, tops.

He cleared this throat before addressing the waiting guests. "I suspect that my grandmother has been saving up a lifetime of stories, waiting to bring them out when my daughter is born, to teach her all the ways that she can make my life miserable. Or I should say, *our* lives miserable. Sloane, I suppose I'm lucky that you didn't hear any of these tales before you foolishly agreed to marry me. It's too late now! No changing your mind."

Sloane heard the crowd's appreciative chuckles. She felt Ethan's right hand fold over hers. She saw him raise his glass. She heard him say, "I ask each of you to drink to my continued good fortune. May I always be as lucky as I was the day that Sloane Davenport agreed to be my wife."

Sloane looked down at their joined hands. She knew that the guests would think that she was being shy, demure. She suspected that even Ethan would think that she was simply overcome with nerves at being the center of this spectacle. As their daughter delivered a strong kick, though, Sloane realized that she was counting the seconds until she could escape.

Margaret's birthday. Stock transfer agreement.

Zach's words kept pounding through her brain. Her engagement, her pending marriage, Ethan saying that he loved her—it was all one grand charade. It was all a business deal. Her hand in marriage. Margaret's stock for Hartwell Genetics. AFAA left out in the cold.

Not entirely in the cold. The foundation would get the consolation prize of Margaret's grand gift. The check that the old woman had written to cover Sloane's Hope Project.

This must be the way that big money did things. I'll scratch your back; you scratch mine. You marry my grandson; I'll give you back your job.

Sloane's head was reeling. With the speeches done, guests surged around them, offering congratulations to Ethan, best wishes to her. Sloane responded with a lifetime of learned politeness, smiling absently, making all the expected replies. The crowd eased between her and Ethan, and Sloane was relieved to have some space, to get away from the complete *awareness* that she felt whenever he stood next to her.

Ethan grimaced as he finished shaking hands with a congressman from South Carolina. He'd somehow agreed to meet the man for breakfast the following week, to discuss the possibility of opening a manufacturing plant just outside of Charleston.

By the time Ethan managed to shrug off the politician, he realized that Sloane was halfway across the room. She was steadier on her feet now, but his heart twisted in his chest as he saw just how vulnerable she looked. Her graceful shoulders seemed so inadequate to the task of navigating the crowd....

He took two steps to follow her, ready to spirit her away to the Town Car and home and a restorative dinner of scrambled eggs and toast, alone in the privacy of their kitchen. Before he could follow through, though, he heard his grandmother's voice, piercing the tangle of party conversation. "Ethan, darling. There's someone I want you to meet."

He shot one more look toward Sloane's disappearing back. She must be heading down the hallway, toward Grandmother's living quarters. Sloane could put her feet up there, take a break from the chaos of the party. He'd rescue her soon enough.

He remembered to curve his lips into a smile before he turned back to the newest business connection his grandmother was presenting.

Sloane reached the elevator, relieved that her escape had gone undetected. She'd been prepared with an excuse for anyone who stopped her—she just needed to lie down for a few minutes, put her feet up in one of Margaret's grand guest rooms. No one had noticed when Sloane left the living room, though. No one cared. The wheels of big business just kept on turning.

She clutched her handbag close to her side as the elevator descended all twelve stories. She was grateful that she'd brought the purse; all too often in the past couple of weeks, she had let herself depend on Ethan entirely, let herself trust him to be ready with tips, with credit cards, with whatever financial arrangements were required.

That night, though, for Margaret's party, she'd wanted to be perfect. She'd needed a lipstick for mid-party touch-ups, and a couple of acetaminophen in case the crowd brought on a headache. It had been second nature for her to slip her wallet into her sleek clutch purse as well.

Second nature. And good fortune.

Sloane crossed the empty lobby, pleased that she

didn't encounter any late-arriving guests. Not that any of them would even recognize her. Sloane was just a prop for the bigger drama that was unfolding upstairs. Just a conveniently needy woman for Ethan, someone he could use to meet Margaret's birthday ultimatum.

She had to say, Ethan was an excellent actor. He knew exactly what to say to keep Sloane by his side. He hadn't planned on their fighting on Independence Day. He hadn't meant to endanger his deal. That was when he'd finally confessed his so-called love—when she had most threatened his boardroom arrangement. And she had fallen for it, hook, line and sinker.

Sloane had been a business proposition, all along. A cold, hard bargain, driven to preserve some insane family obligation.

The thought flashed through her mind that she was wrong. She knew Ethan better than that. They understood each other more completely. But then she remembered how he had reacted to Daisy's illness. He had been perfectly capable, perfectly *comfortable,* cutting the little dog out of his life entirely. He could turn his emotions on and off like a spigot.

He had lied to Sloane every single day for the past two months, every instant that he let her believe that he was giving up his Bachelor-of-the-Year ways for her, for their daughter. *Truth. Respect. Partnership.* Those were just words for him. Meaningless syllables.

For the first time since Sloane had stood on the Kennedy Center terrace, she was one hundred percent grateful that she had insisted on maintaining *some* distance from Ethan—physical, if not emotional. How much worse would it have been to hear Zach's words, if she and Ethan had spent the past two months in the intimacy of a physical relationship? How much worse would it be to realize that he had lied with his body as well as his words?

Approaching the heavy glass door to the outside, Sloane realized that Ethan's driver would pull into the circular driveway the instant that he saw her pause on the threshold. She never gave the guy a chance, though. Instead, she exited as if she had a distinct destination, turning to her right and rushing toward the sidewalk without any hint of hesitation. With any luck at all, the driver wouldn't recognize her in the few seconds before she slipped into twilight shadows. He wouldn't be able to report to Ethan. Couldn't turn her in.

She walked two blocks before she got to busy Connecticut Avenue. Three taxis passed by her raised hand, already ferrying passengers to their own destinations. The fourth one, though, pulled to a stop. She opened the back door reflexively, settled into the seat, fastened the belt.

"Where to?" the driver asked, glancing at her in the rearview mirror.

Sloane moved her purse onto her lap. Her wallet held the five hundred-dollar bills that Ethan had left for her that first morning, the day that he had tracked her down in her dingy basement apartment. She had intended to use them on a wedding present for him, buying him something sweet and sentimental, something that marked some inside joke that only they could share.

Well, there was nothing sweet or sentimental about their wedding.

Unable to think of a destination, increasingly aware of the driver's exasperation, Sloane said the first thing that popped into her mind. "Take me to the Eastern Hotel, please."

Chapter Ten

Sloane huddled against the headboard, the snowy-white hotel duvet pulled up to her chin. It had been easy enough to get a room. Not the penthouse suite that she and Ethan had shared; her cash wouldn't stretch that far, by any means. But a regular room, with a king-size bed and a view of Pennsylvania Avenue, America's Main Street. A retreat.

She'd slipped off her uncomfortable shoes and hung her party dress in the closet. The rich terry-cloth robe, so thoughtfully provided by the Eastern, felt like a memory of the childhood she'd never had, a whisper of comfort as she wrapped herself inside its modest warmth. Despite the robe, though, her teeth had started to chatter.

She'd adjusted the thermostat in the room, turning off the whispering air conditioner. She'd run her hands under the hot water faucet in the bathroom, holding them in the stream until they turned red. She'd looked longingly at the Jacuzzi tub, but she knew that she couldn't indulge in a steaming hot bath. She had to protect her daughter. Had to do what was right for both of them.

It had been so easy to slip into the dream represented by Ethan Hartwell. So easy to believe that she could live in a nice house, surrounded by nice things. She could talk to kind people like James. She could eat gourmet breakfasts, work in a complete library, surrounded by wonder-filled books.

But she wasn't supposed to be that woman. She wasn't supposed to have that sort of good fortune.

Sloane Davenport was a misfit kid, a foster child. She was the girl without a real family, without real friends.

That's what had happened with Ethan, she now realized. She'd been so eager to make things perfect. So eager to live the life she desired. She'd told herself stories, told herself *lies.* Made herself believe lies told to her. He loved her. Ha. Any idiot could see that Ethan Hartwell would never be interested in *her,* not in the long run. Not when he had every model and actress in the world to choose from. Not when he could buy whatever companionship he desired.

She closed her eyes and shook her head. It had all seemed so *real.* In the darkness behind her eyelids, she could see Ethan leaning over her. She could feel his lips on hers, teasing, taunting, seeking admission to the heat of her mouth. She could feel his fingers, raising heart-trembling reactions from her flesh. She could smell the pine scent of him, the fragrance unique to the man she had loved.

No.

None of it had been real. Not when Ethan had first told Sloane that he loved her. Not when he'd brought back the joyous news of their daughter's health. Not when he'd given her the engagement ring. It had all been a game, a play, a performance put on for Margaret's benefit. He had always known, in the back of his mind, that he was working to meet his grandmother's ultimatum. He had always been lying to Sloane.

Forget about *truth*. Forget about *respect*. And don't even mention *partnership*.

Sloane forced herself to take a calming breath. Another. Another.

Maybe she was being ridiculous. Maybe she was making the proverbial mountain out of a molehill.

But she couldn't get past one simple fact: Ethan could have told her about Margaret's demands at any time. He could have shared the truth. They could have laughed about it together. If their relationship were real, wouldn't Ethan have done that? Wouldn't he have trusted her?

Zach had saved Sloane from a lifetime of misery. Her lips twisted into a grim smile. Perhaps she should pay Zach for his time. Whatever astronomical hourly wage the lawyer commanded, it couldn't be too much, given the value of the lesson he had taught.

As if Sloane had two cents to pay a high-priced lawyer.

She curled her hands into fists. Everything had *seemed* so much better. Sloane had enjoyed a roof over her head, food on the table, medical care for herself and her unborn daughter. She had looked forward to her new job at AFAA, to the fruition of all the hours she'd spent on the Hope Project.

She could never take that job now. She'd been a fool even to consider meeting Lionel Hampton for lunch. The job was as tainted as all the rest of it—a treat dangled by Margaret, to lure Sloane into the bizarre web of Hartwell family deceit.

Miserable, Sloane reached for her purse on the nightstand. She dug out her cell phone, thumbed through the last few entries until she reached Mr. Hampton's phone number. She pressed the button to reply to his call. One ring. Two. Three. His voice mail picked up halfway through the fourth ring.

She didn't pay attention to his authoritarian message, didn't bother to hear how sorry he was to have missed her call, how she could reach his assistant. Instead, she waited for the mechanical beep, and then she said, "Mr. Hampton, this is Sloane Davenport. I'm afraid I won't be able to meet with you next week after all. Thank you for your interest in my project. I hope that the foundation does well in the future."

She hung up before she could change her mind.

After that, she didn't have anything more to do. There was no one else to call. No one to talk to. No one to share the mess she'd made of her life.

She pulled the robe closer around her body, slashing the belt tight with a series of tight motions. Her teeth started to chatter again as she pulled the duvet up to her ears.

No one could find her here. She'd paid with cash. She was anonymous. She could sleep until morning, until she needed to check out, until she needed to leave the Eastern and figure out a new place to live, a new way to find food, clothes. Tomorrow would be soon enough for all of that. She started sobbing, well before she managed to fall asleep.

She woke to the sound of pounding on the door.

She couldn't remember where she was. The room was dark, so dark. This wasn't the bright guest suite of Ethan's home.

She rubbed her hand across her face, rasping her skin with loops of terry cloth. Memory flooded back to her; she was in the Eastern, hiding from everyone, from everything. She blinked hard and glanced toward the window. She could see that it was bright outside; a chink in the blackout curtains revealed summer sunshine.

The pounding began again, and she swung her feet over the edge of the bed. She fumbled for the reading lamp on the nightstand, took three tries to find the switch. Dull yellow light washed across the room.

Her mouth was dry; she tried to figure out what she would say to whoever had awakened her. She must have slept past checkout time. She hoped that the hotel wouldn't charge her for a second day. She had no way of paying. Not without using Ethan's credit card. And she was never going to use Ethan's credit card again.

Abruptly, the noise at the door stopped. Sloane drew a deep breath, grateful for the reprieve. She could take a shower. She could get dressed. She could have a few more minutes before the sanctuary of the Eastern was taken away from her.

In her rush of relief, she almost missed the sound of the key card whispering through the door's lock. A solid *snick,* though, indicated that the mechanism had released. Two men were silhouetted in the cold light that flooded in from the hallway.

Ethan's relief was so sharp that he needed to steady himself against the door frame with one hand. The sight of Sloane stole his breath away, left him literally unable to speak. She stood beside her rumpled bed, clutching her robe closed at the neck. The folds of fabric hid the gentle swell of her belly, protecting her modesty perfectly.

Her hair was mussed, as if she'd had a bad night's

sleep. He could see a faint crease on one cheek. Her eyes were blurry, their sapphire brilliance hidden for once, as if she were still dozing, still dreaming whatever crazy nightmare had brought her to this place.

He turned to the manager, intensely aware of the privacy of this moment, of his need to be alone with the woman who was going to be his wife. "Thank you," he said. "That will be all."

The manager bristled. "Sir, you said that this woman's health is in danger. It is certainly not the policy of the Eastern to burst into guests' rooms unannounced—"

Ethan turned to Sloane. He could see the confusion on her face, the frown that pulled down the corners of her mouth. Taking a single step closer, he could see the faint puffiness beneath her eyes, silent, accusing proof that she'd been crying. "Sloane," he said, and he was astonished to hear his voice break across her name. "Please…"

She blinked, obviously still confused. The manager's thin lips twisted in disdain. "Sir," the man said. "You will leave this room immediately, or I'll be forced to call security." He backed up his threat by setting one firm hand on Ethan's biceps.

Ethan resisted the urge to shrug free. He had to prove that he was here to help Sloane. That she would be safe with him. "Sloane," he said, and this time his throat worked properly. "I spoke with Zach. He told me what he said. That you misunderstood. *Please.*"

Sloane shook her head, more in disbelief than in denial. Now that she was awake, she could see how limited her options were. By the light of day—a new day, when she would owe new fees for the hotel room—she realized just how little she could do to get her life back on track.

She also knew, though, that Ethan wasn't any physical threat to her. From the look on the manager's face, the police might be getting involved at any minute. She found the presence of mind to nod once, to send a grateful smile at the hotel official. "Thank you," she said. "I'll let him stay."

"Madam," the manager said, puffing out his chest. "I assure you that the Eastern takes every guest's safety as a matter of utmost concern. I would never have let this man in here if he had not convinced me that it was a matter of life or death, that your physical safety was endangered at this very moment."

She barely glanced at Ethan. She couldn't bear to look at him. "I understand. He can be very convincing."

"Madam?"

She had to cut him off. Had to stand up for herself. Had to take the first steps down the long road of the rest of her life. "Thank you. I'm not afraid of him. He can stay."

The manager stared at her for a long minute, obviously weighing whether she was making her decision freely and without duress. He must have approved of what he saw, though, because he finally stepped out into the hall. "You can reach me at any time, simply by pressing zero on any hotel phone."

Zero. Just like in Ethan's home.

Sloane nodded her appreciation, then waited for the door to swing closed behind him. She gathered her robe closer about her, stepping back toward the bed, trying to put as much space as possible between Ethan and herself. The silence stretched between them, long and dangerous. She tested a dozen thoughts, tried twenty conversational openings, but nothing was right. Nothing fit.

He read the indecision on her face as clearly as if she were shouting at him. He had to say something, do something to let her know that she *could* trust him, that he hadn't just been making an excuse for the manager. "Thank you," he said, putting solid emotion behind the words.

He glanced at the reading lamp beside the bed, at the feeble pool of light that it spread across the floor. He needed to change that, needed to bring her out of whatever dark place she'd retreated to. "May I?" he asked, nodding toward the window.

She hesitated a moment, but she nodded. He took longer than he needed to, crossing to the curtains. He pulled the shades slowly, giving her time to adjust. Time to grow comfortable with the change.

He turned back to face her, and he caught the tail end of a nervous gesture, of her running her fingers through her hair. The black cascade over her shoulders tightened his throat. He spread his fingers wide, forcing himself to take a steadying breath, to relax, to keep from frightening her further.

"How did you find me?" she asked. What had she done to betray herself? She thought she'd been so careful, purposely avoiding using his credit card, being tracked by his driver.

He nodded toward her cell phone on the nightstand. "Hartwell Genetics security," he said. "You made a call last night, to AFAA. We could trace it from the office."

She swallowed hard. The foundation, catching her once again. She forced herself to meet his eyes. "Ethan, I placed that call to cut my ties. I told the foundation that I wouldn't work for them. Wouldn't take Margaret's money."

He nodded, as if he had expected as much. Nevertheless, he asked, "Why?"

She stared at him, incredulous. "Do you have to ask? I can't work for them. Not when the job is only another round of charity. Not when it's just another manipulation, another way of Margaret reining you in."

"Me?" He sounded astonished, but she refused to be drawn in to another round of his game playing.

"You said that you spoke to Zach. Then you know that he told me all about Margaret's ultimatum. You need to be married by Margaret's birthday or you lose everything. I understand that."

She rubbed her arms, fighting off the deadly chill that nearly made her teeth chatter. She wasn't losing anywhere near as much as Ethan was. Not control over a corporation. Not a family fortune. She was only walking away from luxury that she'd enjoyed for a couple of months.

Of course Ethan had made his choice. Of course he'd agreed to his grandmother's demands, kept them secret in case Sloane even thought of protesting. She couldn't blame him. Wouldn't blame him.

He eyed her steadily. "Sloane, I made my choice. I chose you." He closed the distance between them, standing so close that she could feel the heat from his body, could feel a human warmth that she thought would never be hers again. "I chose you and our daughter."

He made it sound so simple. So easy. She bit her lip, trying desperately to maintain her concentration. "No. If you had truly made up your mind, you would have told me about Margaret's demands. You wouldn't have waited for some lawyer to betray your secret. You would have shared the truth."

As soon as she said the words, he saw the piece of

paper she had created, her carefully folded marriage manifesto. *Truth. Respect. Partnership.* For the first time, he completely understood how deeply he had betrayed her. He had failed on every one of her counts.

Truth. He had lied by omission, every single time that he chose not to tell her about Grandmother's demands.

Respect. He had treated her as if she were an incompetent, a child, a fool, someone who could never understand the real pressures in his life.

Partnership. He had never let her be his equal, never relied on her to stand beside him, to work with him, together, to solve the problem of Grandmother's demands.

He could try to explain the twisted way his mind had worked. He could try to tell her that he had been working to protect her, to keep her safe from emotional harm. He could repeat the words that he had taken so long to say, reiterate the simple, unassailable fact that he loved her. That she was the one woman he had ever loved.

His excuse wasn't good enough. His reasoning was completely flawed. She had given him a rulebook, a simple formula, and he had utterly, completely failed. He wanted to reach out for her, to touch her, to convey the perfect truth of his understanding with the language of their bodies, the only language that he'd ever made work between them. But for now, the only thing that he could do was struggle with unwieldy words.

"Sloane, I should have trusted you. I was wrong in a hundred different ways. You told me, you wrote it down in black and white, and I still didn't understand. I was an idiot, Sloane, but you have to believe me when I tell you that I love you. I love the way you fight for what you believe in. I love the way you build your own life, making it what *you* want it to be. I love the way you make your lists, the way you set all the world's wild, confusing emotions into simple, straightforward words. Trust. Respect. Partnership." His voice broke on the last word, and then he whispered, "I'm a better man when I'm with you, Sloane. Let me be with you. Let me stay with you. Let me love you."

She had to shut her eyes against the sight of him. This was not an Ethan Hartwell she had ever seen before. This was a man who was stripped to his bones, who was bare to the world. "Ethan," she whispered, not trusting herself to say more.

"Sloane." His voice was so husky that she felt the words more than heard them. "Grandmother's birthday doesn't matter. It's just a date. If you want, I'll wait until next year, until June, or whenever you agree to marry me. I don't care about stock transfers, about corporate obligations. If there isn't room for me at Hartwell Genetics, I'll build my own company. *We* will. Please. Just tell me that you will marry me eventually. Not today, not tomorrow, but some day, when you can trust me again. I love you, and I'm begging you. Will you be my wife, sometime, in the future, with no more games between us?"

Her heart stopped beating. Her breath froze in her lungs. She was suspended in a cocoon of silence, of space. All of her fears shimmered on the edge of her vision, all of her dark thoughts whispered at the very limit of her hearing. Ethan stared at her, perfectly still, hope indelibly written across his features.

The baby stirred inside her, reminding her to speak. Ethan had said everything, had confessed everything, had made every argument he could ever make. And in the end, she had to embrace the essential truth: she loved him. She loved him as much as he loved her.

"Yes," she whispered.

He crushed her to him. Apparently freed by her acceptance, his body moved to enfold her, to gather her close, to show her that she was his and his alone. His kiss was devastating, igniting her lips, sparking across her tongue. She clutched at his back, wrapped her fingers in his hair, pulling him closer, deeper.

The ice that had bound her shattered into a million shards, bursting with all the force of frantic, pent-up love. Fire thrust into her belly, making her heart kick hard in her chest. She moaned against his lips, barely managing to form his name in her gasping desire.

She slipped her fingers into the waistband of his trousers, pulling him toward her, toward the rumpled bed. As she fumbled at his already loosened tie, she realized that he was still wearing the suit he'd worn to their engagement party. He'd spent the entire night seeking her, tracking her, desperate for her; he hadn't gone home, hadn't taken any creature comfort.

She smothered her remorse as she pulled off his shirt, laughing as his eager fingers helped her. The laughter turned to a gasp of shock as he stripped away the belt from her robe.

He buried his face in the hollow of her neck, nuzzling the tender flesh with such perfect attention that she was forced to squirm away, to pull back, gasping for air. Her hands found his, though, and she pulled him to the bed, tugging him down beside her.

Her robe slipped open as she tumbled into the sheets, and he lost no time measuring the perfect flesh of her body. He was overwhelmed by the need to know her, to feel her, to understand every inch of her. His lips followed his fingertips in exploration as he traced the dark circles that accented her breasts, as he discovered the perfect beads waiting for his attention.

She writhed beneath him, tightening his groin. He shifted, trying to maintain contact with her sweet flesh, trying to fill his lungs with the honeysuckle scent of her, with the warmth that radiated from every exposed inch of her.

The power of his need was simply too great, too painful. He tore at his trousers, kicked them off, banishing them to the floor with a grateful gasp.

That relief, though, was short-lived. Sloane reached out to help him, edging her slim fingers beneath the elastic waist of his boxers. The touch of her hands on the full length of him nearly made Ethan shout her name; he had to bury his face in the soft valley between her breasts, had to smother his instinctive cries. He forced himself to breathe deeply, to calm his raging need, to ease the throbbing pressure that threatened to convulse him.

Sloane laughed in pure delight. She had never imagined that she could have this much power over a man, that she could bring such a powerful creature completely under her sway. Feeling wicked, she traced one fingernail from the forest of tight curls to his velvet tip, rejoicing as Ethan's entire body shuddered.

He tried to pull away, but she only let him get far enough that she could strip off the last garment between them, that she could send his boxers to the floor with the rest of his clothes. He succumbed to her decision, and she thought she was in control, until he wrapped his arms around her, rolling her so that his back was cushioned by the mattress, so that she was sprawled across his chest, her robe finally lost in the chaos of the sheets.

He took advantage of their new position, raising his head to suckle at her right breast. The touch of his lips on her tight nipple sent waves of heat rolling over her body, ripples of pure sensation that drew her in, focusing her on a single circle of pure, flawless pleasure. She thought that she'd never felt anything as wondrous, anything as perfect, and then he shifted his attention to her other breast. Whimpering, she threw her head back, nearly overwhelmed by the intensity of the feeling he raised within her.

With velvet tongue and satin lips, he fed the fire within her. Red-orange-gold flames flowed through her body, eddied in her veins, pooled deep inside her core. Backfires were kindled by his fingertips digging into her waist, by the firm grip of his hands as he held her steady, held her close, locked her in to the pure pleasure he delivered.

Overcome by the intensity, she tried to arch away from him, tried to give her body the cool break that she thought she needed. He merely doubled his attention, though, adding tiny nips from his perfect teeth to accent the sensations that flooded through her breasts. She shuddered at the new sensation, crying out in surprise. The solid touch of his palms against her flanks reminded her of the child inside her, of the daughter they had created, of the unexpected, perfect beauty they had shared months before. His hands were anchors, pulling her closer to him, securing her body to his.

One more tug of his teeth, one more tickle with his tongue, and she crashed over the precipice she'd known was terrifyingly close. She cried out his name, drowning in the sudden whirlpool that roared through her core. The entire world around her disappeared; she was reduced to the brilliant fire that he sparked inside her, billowing wave after billowing wave of endless, mindless heat.

In that moment outside of time, Ethan thought that his

heart might break from the beauty he saw before him. Sloane's hair surrounded her face like a midnight halo. Her eyes were closed, hiding away the brilliant intelligence that had drawn him to her in the first place. Her lips had tightened into a perfect circle in the instant before he gave her the release that she craved; now, her mouth was relaxed, swollen, begging him to drink as deeply as he dared.

He felt the aftershocks ripple through her body, the shuddering descent as she returned to awareness, to reality. The iron muscles of her fingers, her hands, her wrists unlocked, and she telegraphed the final waves of her sweet tension to the broad muscles of his chest.

That secret message, those unspoken words, reminded his proud flesh that he had sacrificed for her pleasure, that he had denied himself even the faintest hope of release. His body shifted of its own accord, and her eyes opened wide, suddenly filled with understanding.

"Ethan," she breathed.

He couldn't keep from touching her. He couldn't restrain himself from brushing the hair off her face, from tracing the delicate line of her lips as she hesitated. He'd hurt her. Hurt her in ways that he hadn't understood, that he'd never intended. He would spend the rest of his life making that up to her, giving her whatever she wanted, whatever she needed, now that she'd agreed to stay with him forever. "Yes, love," he said, lifting one of her hands from his chest, brushing his lips across the sweet silk of her palm.

"I want to feel you," she said, holding his gaze. She set each word between them with perfect precision, just as he had once predicted she would, on the night he had proposed. She wasn't asking for a kiss. She wasn't asking for simple physical release. "All of you," she said. "Like we did before, before all of our misunderstandings, all of the confusion. Please, Ethan. I need you inside me, now."

He had no intention of making her ask again.

His arms were firm around her as he pulled her to his side, as he shifted so that she felt his body against hers, his legs stretched beside her own. The rasp of the hair on his thighs awoke new sensations in her, stirring her to an awareness she would have thought impossible only a few heartbeats before. She thought that he had shown her all the pleasure of her physical self, that he had taught her everything she could enjoy, but now she knew his lessons were only beginning.

As if he sensed her uncertainty, he kissed her. This was not a kiss of passion, not a kiss of endless, reeling sensation. Instead, it was a pure bonding, a seal of all the promises they'd ever made to each other, of all the vows they'd ever taken, ever were going to take. There was a sweetness on his lips, an infinite tenderness, and she knew that he had never meant to hurt her, would never hurt her again. That kiss made tears rise in her eyes, happy tears, joyful tears, and he wiped the moisture from her cheeks with a gentle touch.

Still holding her gaze, he lowered his hand to her waist. He found her damp folds without hesitation, stroking once, twice, coaxing her to open. She shifted her hips, responding to his call, biting her lip at the sensations he stirred within her.

Slowly, with perfect deliberation, he ran a finger over the most tender pearl between her thighs. Pure sensation jolted through her, arching her spine against him, driving her to seek immediate release.

He shook his head, though, smiling with the intensity of an explorer about to discover a whole new world. His fingers touched her again, ignited her again, and she closed her eyes against the sheer physicality of the sensation.

"No," he whispered, and the command was as gentle as the last kiss they'd shared. "Watch me. I want to see your eyes."

She swallowed hard, wondering if she dared. Another pass of his fingers. Another blast of pure, grasping pleasure. A new energy, a new force, as she managed to maintain eye contact, as she read his promise of eternal, perfect devotion.

Knowing that she was ready, knowing that he had primed her to take the length of him without harm to herself, to her body, to the precious child that she bore, he raised himself above her. Her gaze was steady. Trusting. She was ready for this new life between them, the new shape of love between their bodies, between their souls.

For just an instant, he hovered, feeling the sweet softness of her entrance, sensing the magical need that chimed through her veins and sang to his flesh. And then, he eased himself inside.

He moved as slowly as he could, giving her time to adjust, to accept, to envelop the full length of him. The tightness of her feminine muscles nearly undid him; he would have lost control, if not for her pure, unshuttered gaze. His hips met hers, and they were joined completely, in perfect balance, in perfect trust.

Careful, watching her for any sign of pain, he started to withdraw. Her fingers scrabbled on his back, coaxing him forward with a new urgency. He yielded to her silent request, dipping back into the honeyed sweetness of her core.

She felt the rhythm grow between them, the ways their bodies adjusted to each other. Heat poured from him into her, spiraling deeper inside, winding past all of her inhibitions, any lingering thoughts of right and wrong. Overwhelmed by the sensation, by her emotions, she closed her eyes, the better to concentrate on the power expanding between them.

"Sloane," he whispered, summoning her back. His fingers traced the line of her jaw, and she forced her eyes open, locked on to the steady agate of his gaze.

She'd thought that she could not find release again, not so soon after the utter dissolution of her body. He worked his magic, though, as if he'd known her flesh forever; he tightened the muscles of her belly, of her thighs. He filled her inner channel, drawing her closer, deeper, further inside an aching tunnel of need. One long stroke, deeper than any before. Another. One last thrust, and she was shuddering, toppling over a cliff of pure, rolling sensation, clenching every muscle in her body before opening up in blinding release.

He saw the wonder in her eyes as she reached her cliff, saw the moment just before he let her go, saw the instant that her body was flooded with exquisite freedom. He rode out the storm beneath him, giving her every last instant of pleasure, willing himself to hold back, to deliver more, to share every heartbeat that he could.

When the storm was finally fading, though, she shifted her hips, jolting him to a new level of awareness. He had restrained himself for so long that only the slightest movement was necessary to hurtle him toward his own edge. Catching a single ragged breath, he pulled back, nearly deserting the heaven of her ready core. Then, he plunged deep inside her, one last thrust unlocking all of his reserve, freeing him to fill her.

He nearly broke his own rule then, nearly closed his eyes, but the sparkling joy on Sloane's face kept him fully aware. He clutched her shoulders as his power pulsed out of him, drawing her closer, closer, never losing the lifeline of her gaze.

She held him until the end, overcome by the pure physicality of the life force that they shared. At last, he collapsed beside her, his breath as rapid as if he'd run a marathon. She kissed him, letting her lips tremble against his. She pulled his arm around her, relishing the weight, the power, the unbroken security.

She knew that they would be together now. They would follow through with the mechanics of marriage, with a license, with vows. But they had more than that. They had the power of true love, of shared destiny. They had kindled a new life, a new person, to symbolize their joined and perfect love.

Sighing, she burrowed close to his side. And then, they slept.

Epilogue

Ethan watched with pride as Sloane adjusted Emma's blanket. The baby didn't stir, even though she was the centerpiece of attention.

"Ready, Gran?" he asked, turning to Margaret Hartwell.

"Ready," she affirmed. The photographer swooped into action, moving in with his camera, directing the matriarch as no other man dared to do. He ordered the proud great-grandmother to turn her head, to tilt her chin, to gaze down at the infant in her arms.

Ethan stepped back, awed at how readily the old tyrant complied. Sloane was watching, a smile on her lips. He settled his arm around her waist, drawing her in close to his side. Sloane sighed and said, "I can't believe how good she's being."

"Gran always did rise to the occasion," he said, with purposeful misunderstanding.

"Ethan!" Sloane whirled toward him in disapproval, but settled for a quick kiss as reprimand.

Other photos had already been taken, one formal composition, with Ethan and Sloane together, looking down at their perfect child. Another, with Gran holding the baby, while Ethan and Sloane gazed down from behind her thronelike chair. A series of Sloane holding a wakeful Emma, maternal joy radiating with a purity so brilliant it had captured Ethan's breath and he'd needed to look away. A portrait of the entire family, including Daisy, who had sat at perfect canine attention, through a half-dozen camera flashes.

Sloane watched as the photographer turned Margaret to another angle, focused his soft floodlights to drive away shadows. She whispered to Ethan, "I can't believe how many he's taking! It's been hours!"

He smiled indulgently. "Not as long as he would have taken to capture our wedding, if you'd let me give you a real ceremony."

She caught her lip between her teeth at his teasing tone. They'd never had this conversation; it hadn't seemed necessary at any point in the past four and a half months, since they'd emerged from the Eastern Hotel and gone directly to a justice of the peace in Virginia. "Do you really care? Did you really want a full wedding?"

He laughed, loudly enough that Daisy scurried to his side. The photographer cast a quick scowl in their direction, and Sloane meekly pulled them toward the back of the room, away from the busy work of capturing the perfect portrait. One quick hand command guaranteed that Daisy followed suit, staying out of the thick of things.

When they were safe in the privacy of the corner, Ethan slipped his hands around Sloane's waist, drew her close with a firmness that promised more, that reminded her precisely how well they fit together, how perfect they were for each other. "The only thing that matters to me, Mrs. Hartwell, is that you agreed to marry me. That you signed the paper, in front of the justice of the peace and two legal witnesses. That you wear my ring. And that you rock our daughter to sleep at night, with me standing right beside you."

She sighed and settled her cheek against his chest. She could hear his heart beating through the fabric of his shirt, a steady reminder of the power of his love. As if to horn in on the sweet domestic scene, though, Daisy raised a paw to scratch at Ethan's leg. At the same time, Sloane and Ethan both commanded, "Down!" The dog dropped to the floor immediately.

Sloane laughed before she looked up at Ethan. "You know," she said. "I have a confession to make."

His smile was easy. "I can't wait to hear this."

"It's about Daisy. When we first got her, when she was just a puppy, I hired a trainer to come out to the house. I wanted Daisy to be perfect, so that you'd fall in love with her as much as I had." She was startled by the volume of Ethan's laugh. "Wait!" she exclaimed. "It wasn't *that* funny. I mean, I did a decent job, didn't I?"

"A decent job," he finally said, but he shook his head as if he didn't believe her.

"What? She sits when we tell her to. And she knows *come* and *stay* and *down*."

Ethan looked fondly at the dog. Daisy, for her part, was cocking her head at an angle, glancing between her two humans as if they were creatures of great mystery. Ethan said, "But she's not much good at *heel*."

Sloane frowned. "We tried. The trainer and I just couldn't get her motivated to stay by my side."

"I didn't have any better luck myself."

"What?" Sloane took a step away, even as Ethan started to laugh again.

"I hired my own trainer. I worked on the same commands. I wanted to show you that I believed in Daisy. That I understood she had a future with us."

The dog chose that moment to spring to her feet, overcome by the obvious good cheer of her master and mistress. Sloane said in disbelief, "Then she managed to wrangle double treats from us, to master the exact same tricks."

"She's smarter than we ever thought, isn't she?"

Before Sloane could respond, her cell phone rang. She jumped at the intrusion but quickly plucked it out of her bag. One glance at the number, and she shook her head.

"Take it," Ethan said.

"This is family time! It's Margaret's birthday."

"Take it," he said again, and she complied, her smile letting him know just how eager she was to answer the call.

"Sloane Hartwell," she said, after pushing the button that completed the connection.

Ethan watched as Sloane nodded. She found her handbag, fished out a pad of paper, a pen. Bright spots of color accented her cheeks, and her eyes sparkled as she mustered her arguments. "No," she said, stepping out to the hallway. "If the foundation is serious about implementing the Hope Project, it's going to have to…" Her voice trailed away as she closed the door behind her.

At last, the photographer finished with his grandmother. Ethan stepped forward to take the baby, marveling at the way a month-old child could sleep through any disturbance. "There, Gran," he said. "You've had your way, once again. You've got your pictures of Emma."

The old woman spared a fond smile for the baby before she leveled her hazel eyes on him. The determination there was utterly familiar; he'd seen it in his own mirror, every day of his life. "I think that family photos were a perfectly reasonable request for a birthday present. It's not every day that someone turns eighty, after all. Besides, you know I only do what I think is best for those I love."

Ethan heard the familiar acerbic note beneath her words. "Of course, Gran. Everything you do is good for someone else."

"You can't complain about the rules I set for you." Her gaze was a direct challenge.

He wanted to argue. He wanted to tell her that she'd been headstrong, unreasonable. He wanted to say that she'd had no business interfering with his personal life, setting deadlines, tying him to an arbitrary timetable.

But when he looked down at his daughter, he knew that such a complaint was meaningless. He couldn't be happier with the way things had turned out. He wouldn't change a thing.

Nevertheless, he couldn't let Gran think that he was growing soft. "You had no right—"

"No right to make you sit up and pay attention?" She cut him off, and he could see now that she had planned this confrontation. She knew precisely what she wanted to say.

"You treated me like a business venture," he protested.

"One that needed a tight rein," she said sourly. "One that had to be brought into line." Emma chose that moment to squirm in her blanket, to stretch out her arms before settling back to sleep. Ethan was surprised at the stark love that he found on his grandmother's face. He was even more startled by her words. "I knew that you needed this, darling. I knew that you were too afraid to step forward on your own. You needed me to push you."

"Over a cliff," he said wryly.

"Into the arms of a good woman," she retorted.

"Who is going into whose arms?" Sloane asked, gliding in from the hallway.

Margaret looked at her, those hazel Hartwell eyes bright with mischief. "I was just telling my boneheaded grandson that his grandmother is a wise and wonderful woman."

Sloane looked at Ethan. She could see echoes of disagreement on his face, hints of some argument that he'd planned on voicing. Now, though, he merely shook his head, his lips curling up in a resigned smile. When he gazed down at his daughter, that expression transformed, became a look of wonder, of sheer fascination. "Listen to her, Emma," he said. "One day all that Hartwell wisdom will be yours."

Still cradling the baby, he held out one hand to Sloane. As she laced her fingers between his and drew close to look at their daughter, she knew that her life could never be more perfect. "Listen to your father, little Emma," she said, brushing a fingertip against the infant's cheek. "Listen to the entire family who loves you so much." Daisy gave one sharp bark of agreement, as if she understood every single human word.

* * * * *

Harlequin®

COMING NEXT MONTH

Available August 30, 2011

SPECIAL EDITION®

REQUEST YOUR FREE BOOKS!

2 FREE NOVELS PLUS 2 FREE GIFTS!

SPECIAL EDITION

Life, Love & Family

New York Times *and* USA TODAY *bestselling author*
Maya Banks presents a brand-new miniseries

PREGNANCY & PASSION

When four irresistible tycoons face
the consequences of temptation.

Book 1—ENTICED BY HIS FORGOTTEN LOVER

Available September 2011 from Harlequin® Desire®!

Rafael de Luca had been in bad situations before. A crowded ballroom could never make him sweat.

These people would never know that he had no memory of any of them.

He surveyed the party with grim tolerance, searching for the source of his unease.

At first his gaze flickered past her, but he yanked his attention back to a woman across the room. Her stare bored holes through him. Unflinching and steady, even when his eyes locked with hers.

Petite, even in heels, she had a creamy olive complexion. A wealth of inky-black curls cascaded over her shoulders and her eyes were equally dark.

She looked at him as if she'd already judged him and found him lacking. He'd never seen her before in his life. Or had he?

He cursed the gaping hole in his memory. He'd been diagnosed with selective amnesia after his accident four months ago. Which seemed like complete and utter bull. No one got amnesia except hysterical women in bad soap operas.

With a smile, he disengaged himself from the group

around him and made his way to the mystery woman.

She wasn't coy. She stared straight at him as he approached, her chin thrust upward in defiance.

"Excuse me, but have we met?" he asked in his smoothest voice.

His gaze moved over the generous swell of her breasts pushed up by the empire waist of her black cocktail dress.

When he glanced back up at her face, he saw fury in her eyes.

"Have we *met?*" Her voice was barely a whisper, but he felt each word like the crack of a whip.

Before he could process her response, she nailed him with a right hook. He stumbled back, holding his nose.

One of his guards stepped between Rafe and the woman, accidentally sending her to one knee. Her hand flew to the folds of her dress.

It was then, as she cupped her belly, that the realization hit him. She was pregnant.

Her eyes flashing, she turned and ran down the marble hallway.

Rafael ran after her. He burst from the hotel lobby, and saw two shoes sparkling in the moonlight, twinkling at him.

He blew out his breath in frustration and then shoved the pair of sparkly, ultrafeminine heels at his head of security.

"Find the woman who wore these shoes."

Will Rafael find his mystery woman?
Find out in Maya Banks's passionate new novel
ENTICED BY HIS FORGOTTEN LOVER
Available September 2011 from Harlequin® Desire®!